DEAD BEFORE I DO

A MADDIE SWALLOWS MYSTERY
BOOK 3

KAT BELLEMORE

KB PRESS

ALSO BY KAT BELLEMORE

A NOTE FROM THE AUTHOR

Before the Maddie Swallows mystery series came to be, I had written nearly two complete small town romance series. *Borrowing Amor* is my first and takes place in New Mexico. The second takes place in the small Californian coastal town of Starlight Ridge.

I love both.

But mystery has been calling my name for some time. I'm especially drawn to mysteries that have quirky characters and make me just as invested in their lives as I am in solving the crime. Books like Richard Osman's *The Thursday Murder Club*, and TV shows like *Psych* and *Monk*, come to mind.

When making the decision to start writing cozy mystery, I knew I wouldn't be leaving romance entirely, and I also knew that I didn't want to leave my characters.

There is more to these towns and the people in them than first meets the eye.

Which is why you now get to experience these lovely towns from a completely different perspective. One that now includes murder and suspicion, in addition to light-hearted humor.

And the characters you knew and loved from the romance series? They are now side characters, helping my sleuth on her journey.

Dead Before I Do is the third book in the Maddie Swallows mystery series. I hope you enjoy reading it as much as I had writing it. Because in writing mystery, I have found where my heart is.

Important Note: Your favorite characters do NOT die. Just in case you were worried.

"Happy birthday, Lilly," I heard Flash sing out. Which instigated a scream and then yelling for him to get out of her room.

I smiled from where I still lay in bed, struggling to wake. I didn't normally sleep in on weekends, but I was having trouble getting up today. Maybe because I was putting off the inevitable.

My little girl had gone and grown up, and today was her eighteenth birthday.

I wasn't sure what to do with that.

Because of her early birthday, Lilly still had most of her senior year left, but that didn't change the fact that she was now researching colleges and planning her future. She wanted to be a film director and was looking at a couple of schools that could provide a certification that would allow her to work background on movies while she got her foot in the door.

Grown-up stuff.

I lay in bed, knowing I needed to run over to the diner to pick up her birthday breakfast, but then that would make it real.

Flash burst into my room. He wore a clown wig and held a can of Silly String, some of which already clung to his wig. A sign hung around his neck, proclaiming him the birthday clown.

Ava, our cat, burst in after him, Silly String draping from her, like she'd just received the wrong end of Flash's birthday decorating. She jumped on my bed and to the dresser, then ran around the room and back out again, as if the Silly String were chasing her.

I tried not to laugh, but that cat terrorized me so often, it was difficult to feel bad for the poor thing.

"I know she's eighteen now," Flash said, not seeming to have registered the cat. "But she's still acting like a child—like my feelings don't matter. All I wanted was to do something special for her, and did you hear how she treated me?"

I sat up and eyed his finger that still rested on the top of the Silly String can, as if ready to push the trigger at a moment's notice.

"Don't you dare shoot me with that stuff," I threatened, though I doubted it came across as menacing, considering I was half-laughing when I said it.

Flash looked at the can, as if he was surprised he was still holding it. "Oh, no. This isn't for you."

"Did you already spray your sister as a morning wakeup call?" I asked, still eyeing the can as I pulled myself from bed.

Flash nodded briskly. "Yes. It was fantastic. Everything a birthday wakeup should be. But you know what she did as thanks? She leaped from her bed, grabbed the can, and sprayed me. Then she pushed me out of her room and threw the can after me. The nerve!"

Oh, my Flash. My dear, dear Flash.

"I hate to break it to you," I said, "but people—especially teenage girls—don't tend to love when they are woken up early on their birthday. Particularly when they are attacked by a clown."

Flash's lips parted in surprise. "I wasn't attacking her. I was celebrating the momentous occasion. My teenage sister is now officially an adult."

There would be no reasoning with the boy, so I didn't bother arguing with him and said, "Even so, maybe next year you can tone it down a bit."

Flash's expression drooped, like this was not at all how he'd expected the morning to go. As he removed the sign from around his neck, I said, "But you know, I myself love clowns on my birthday."

My son perked up at that. "Really?"

I nodded. "Absolutely. And the more Silly String, the better."

"Awesome!"

The things we do for our kids.

Flash puffed out his chest and walked out the door like he was ready for round two. I hoped for both Lilly's sake and his that he wouldn't follow through with that plan.

I glanced at the clock. It was still early, but my grumbling stomach was begging for food. Cooking hadn't been my forte when working as a psychology professor in the big city. My ex-husband Cameron and I would arrive home late enough each evening that the kids had memorized the take-out menus from every local restaurant.

But after the divorce, and my leaving my job, I had moved the kids to my hometown in southern New Mexico, and things had started to change. Not always for the better —it had been a rough transition. But I could now make spaghetti without overcooking the noodles, and grilled cheese sandwiches without burning them. So, that was something.

A trumpet began playing downstairs.

That couldn't have been either of my children, considering neither of them had ever been interested in picking up an instrument.

Trish.

My roommate, best friend, and former university colleague.

In the two years we'd lived together, though, I'd never heard mention of a trumpet.

After pulling a sweatshirt and jeans on, I made my way to Lilly's room to wish her a happy birthday.

I found her in bed, holding a pillow over her ears.

"Happy birthday," I said.

My daughter flew into a seated position, her hair standing in all directions and a look of horror twisting her usually pretty features.

"Make it stop," she whispered. "If I had known what my first day of adulthood would be like, I would have cracked open a fortune cookie and wished to be seventeen forever. There has been a clown, Silly String, and now what I think is supposed to be 'Happy Birthday' on the trumpet...but it is not. I'm fairly certain Trish hasn't pulled out that instrument since middle school." She winced when Trish hit a particularly harsh note. "All I wanted was a quiet morning. Breakfast from the diner. And to go out with some friends. Was that too much to ask for?"

Yup, it was.

"Sorry, girlie. I know you didn't ask to be born into this family, but you are stuck with crazy town for now and always."

Lilly's expression of horror deepened, and she slid back under her covers, replacing the pillow over her ears. "Tell me when you've arrived with food."

I laughed and made my way downstairs. The music had stopped, but I saw that it was only because Trish was looking through some sheet music, presumably to find her next song.

"That's quite the trumpet you have there," I said, not sure how to tactfully ask her to stop.

Trish glanced up, her hair in two braids, bright green stripes accenting her natural blonde. At least I thought blonde was her natural hair color. She dyed it so often, it was difficult to tell. "Thanks," she said with a smile. "Can you believe that I've brought this thing everywhere I've gone over the last twenty years, without ever actually playing it? I'll admit that I started out a bit rusty with that first song, but it's all coming back to me now. Like riding a bike."

Sure. If you were crashing that bike because you didn't know where the brakes were.

"It seems to really make you happy," I said, trying not to go too far into psychologist mode. As a fellow psychologist, it would take Trish 2.4 seconds to spot my Jedi mind tricks. "Did you want to come to the diner with me to grab breakfast?"

Trish pulled a piece of paper from a stack next to her. "If it's all the same to you, I'd rather keep practicing. I have a couple of decades to make up for."

I hesitated and glanced up the stairs to where Lilly was no doubt still hiding under her pillow. I felt bad, but I just didn't know how to get out of this gracefully. "I'm sure you'll be playing the blues in no time."

Trish beamed as she started into what sounded vaguely like "Chattanooga Choo Choo." I hurried out, praying that Lilly would forgive me.

. . .

THE DINER'S food was not known for its quality, but there were few options in town, and the kids liked it well enough. As long as you knew what to get, and what to stay away from, it was fine.

Or maybe there was something I had been missing all these years.

Because judging by the line at the counter this morning, you'd think it was a Michelin five-star restaurant. I tried to see around to the front, but my view was blocked.

A long wait was fine by me. Better chance that Trish would have finished with her musical encore by the time I returned home.

Except, by the time I was able to order from Melinda, the manager of the diner and a woman known for her short temper, I was so hungry, I ordered twice as much as we needed.

"We'll need two scones. Three chocolatey chocolate muffins," I started. "No, maybe we should make that four. Ugh...I don't know if that will be enough. Let's go with six. Of the chocolatey chocolate muffins. Not the scones."

She frowned as she scribbled something out. "You can just say chocolate muffins. It's the only kind we have."

Yes, I could have. But these were chocolate muffins with chocolate chunks and fudge drizzles. I was fairly certain that without them, the diner would have gone out of business years ago, and it would be an insult to lump them in with every other muffin.

I didn't think Melinda would appreciate my analysis, though, so I pretended I hadn't heard her and scanned the menu taped to the counter in front of me. "I should probably get some biscuits and gravy with that, right? And orange juice. I mean, we have to at least pretend we're going to eat something of substance. And you do have good biscuits and gravy."

"You say that like you're surprised," Melinda said, her attention seemingly elsewhere. "Anything else?"

"No, I think that is it. Unless you think I should get a couple more scones. Flash has been eating a lot lately..."

Melinda ripped the page off her notepad. "Four scones coming up."

"You don't think that's too many? I mean, it's just the four of us for breakfast, and we have the muffins and the—"

Melinda didn't give me the chance to change my mind as she handed the order to her cook. She grabbed a prepared plate at the same time and stepped around me to deliver it to someone in the dining area.

Before she reached their table, however, the sound of shattering ceramic stole her attention, and she frowned. "Seriously? Again?"

After delivering the food, she hurried into the back and reappeared with a broom. Even as the line at the counter grew longer, she moved to the dining room to clean up the mess. I'd thought she had hired help, but it appeared she was on her own this morning.

Daniel, a man who'd moved to Amor not long before I had, slid out of his booth and took the broom from Melinda, proceeding to clean up the ceramic shards. I was impressed, considering he didn't work at the diner, hadn't been the one to break the plate, and was only there for his own breakfast.

Melinda's whole demeanor changed, though, and the relief that washed over her was palpable.

"That was a brave man," someone said from behind me.

I knew that voice.

Benji.

I turned and smiled at the sight of him. His stubble was growing out, giving him a proper beard, and his hat kept the rest of his dirty blond hair at bay. He looked good. In a best friend kind of way. I was unsure if I was allowed to see him as anything else. Since moving back home, things had become…complicated. That was what happened when you started to develop feelings for someone you'd known since preschool.

"I know what you mean," I said, getting my thoughts back on track. "She seems grumpier than usual today."

Benji lowered his voice as we watched Melinda take a phone call in the back, the line at the counter growing even longer.

"From how I hear it, Melinda's upset about Bree getting married. I heard she might not even go to the wedding."

Bree. Why was that name familiar?

My confusion must have been evident because Benji gave me an incredulous look. "Melinda's younger sister?" He paused, as if looking for a hint of recognition, but I had none. "I suppose it makes sense you don't remember her. She's a bit younger than us. And then she left for college and never returned. Same as you."

I tried to ignore the guilty feeling the comment evoked. I didn't think Benji meant anything by it, but it still felt like another person telling me that I'd betrayed the town by pursuing my dreams. By chasing after something that Amor didn't provide. By forgetting everyone I'd left behind.

"Anyway," Benji continued, "she's getting married. It's out at White Sands National Park, though. Not sure if I want to make the trek."

Now I remembered where I'd seen the name—while I'd been visiting my mom with the kids, a wedding announcement had arrived. Which she had promptly thrown in the trash. When I'd questioned her, she'd admitted that she'd never gotten along with Melinda and Bree's parents. Apparently, they'd lived on the opposite side of town as us, creating an unseen division between our families. Even a small place like Amor had its poor side, which was where we had lived. The Garretts had lived in a home triple the size of ours. And according to my mother, the wedding announcement was their way of once again rubbing their successes in her face. Never mind that they'd moved from town a decade earlier, leaving Melinda in charge of the diner. I doubted they had ever given my mom a second thought, and it was more likely they'd sent an announcement to everyone in town.

Benji was saying he hadn't received just an announcement, though. He'd received an invitation.

"What made you so lucky to be invited to the wedding?" I asked.

He waved a hand through the air, like it was inconsequential. "My parents are good friends with their parents. My mom and dad will be out of town, and they asked me to go in their stead."

Okay. That made sense. But jealousy raised its head at the thought of Melinda and Benji at the wedding together. The way she openly flirted with him, even when I was sitting right next to him. Of course, she did that with everyone who came into the diner and made the mistake of being male.

And it wasn't like Benji and I were dating. I often felt like we were moving in that direction, but the trajectory seemed to be two steps forward and one step back. Like something was standing in our way.

My thoughts were cut off when Benji said, "Why don't you go with me?"

I stared. "Sorry?"

Benji was nodding vigorously now. "Yes, that way I can

appease everyone. I can make my appearance but also stave off any unwanted attention. You know how weddings are for us single folk."

No, I didn't know.

My hopes had risen for the briefest of seconds, but then dropped. I wouldn't be a date. I'd be a bodyguard.

"So...I'd be there as protection. An excuse."

"Yes, it's perfect!" Benji grinned, as if he didn't see anything wrong with this.

And as much as I wanted to be annoyed at him for his cluelessness at how that might make me feel, I couldn't help but smile back.

Because Benji had just invited me to go away with him. To a wedding.

My first weekend away from the kids. Ever.

And a way for me to figure out my feelings for this man I'd known my entire life.

Benji was right. It was perfect.

When I returned home, Trish was cleaning Silly String from inside the bell of her trumpet. Apparently, she'd been ambushed shortly after I'd left. She'd laughed it off as one of Flash's pranks, and it seemed she truly didn't know that it was because the kids hadn't been able to take her musical prowess for another minute more.

"You have to go," she said the moment I'd confided that Benji had invited me to Bree's wedding.

I held out my hand to take the rag from her and finish the cleanup job, propelled by my guilt for the unkind thoughts I'd had toward her trumpet.

"I don't even know the woman and barely remember their parents," I said as I scooped a massive pile of Silly String out of the trumpet's bell. Flash hadn't been playing around. "The only one in the family I really know is

Melinda, and I've only seen her smile twice. Ever. Not exactly a wedding I want to be a part of."

"But Benji will be there, and that's the whole point, isn't it?" Trish said. "I can stay back with the kids, no problem. Besides, it would only be for a couple of days."

Benji.

The thought of being alone with him... It both excited and terrified me. How did one figure out how to be more than best friends without completely ruining what we already had?

"My mom will probably drop by a dozen times a day, making sure you haven't managed to burn the place down." I was riddled with anxiety, and my poor brain was coming up with any excuse to get out of it. "And what about my patients?"

Trish and I had opened our own therapy office in town when we'd both left our university jobs, and it was going well. So well, in fact, that we had a month-long waiting list. That was in addition to volunteering a few hours a week with the homeless community.

"The wedding is on Saturday afternoon, right? Go up that morning, come back on Sunday. No harm done." Trish paused. "Of course, your mom is a different matter altogether."

My mother.

Trish and she hadn't gotten along very well since I'd returned to my hometown after a twenty-year absence. Jealousy seemed to be the root of it, because I spent much of my time with my friend and roommate rather than my mom.

That largely had to do with the fact that I could only handle my mother in small doses. I was working on it—I was. But it had been only my mom and me growing up, and those hadn't always been the happiest years of my life.

"You know what, we'll be fine," Trish said, sensing my hesitancy. "It's about time your mother and I learned to see eye to eye. Or at least learned to accept each other's presence. It's a sacrifice for the greater good. You and Benji need this."

I hated that Trish was right and that I was running out of excuses.

"All right," I said. "Looks like I'm going to a wedding."

"You're sure you're going to be all right?" I asked the kids, even as I packed my suitcase. Benji had been thrilled when I'd told him I'd accompany him to the wedding, and he didn't seem to feel at all weird about it.

That was a relief. Mostly.

At least there would be no pressure.

"We'll be fine," Lilly said. "I'm an adult now, and Trish will be here. We'll keep Flash out of trouble."

An adult.

How I longed for the times when my kids had needed me—when I couldn't just take off. It had been inconvenient, but this new reality... It was strange. Difficult in a completely new and different way.

"He's going to be here any minute," Lilly said, browsing my closet. "What are you wearing to the wedding? Because I think you should wear this one." She pulled a sleeveless dress out of my closet. It was chocolate brown and hit just below my knee. It had always been my go-to for fancy events, paired with a pair of cream sandals that tied around my calves, similar to what a Greek goddess might wear.

It hugged me in all the right places, which was why I had chosen a more conservative dress that wasn't nearly as flattering.

Had I done that subconsciously? It seemed I was trying to sabotage anything that might potentially happen this weekend.

"I already have a dress packed," I said, but my voice lacked conviction. Now that I thought about it, it was a dress I'd been contemplating giving away—one that I hadn't worn in years because I really didn't like it.

Lilly handed me the chocolate brown dress. She looked so much older as she held up the lavender dress I'd packed and shook her head. "You hate this one."

I raised a shoulder. "It's not that bad."

"Mom," Lilly said, her voice soft. "We like Benji. You don't need to worry about us. Just go have fun and see where it takes you."

I rummaged in my closet until I found my goddess

sandals. "I'm not worried about you and your brother. I mean, I am, but I see how well you two get along with Benji. It's just that...what if Benji doesn't want anything other than what we are? At times it seems like he's all in, and then he pulls back. I've gone back and forth on the subject myself, and I don't want you guys to get your hopes up."

I zipped up my suitcase and double-checked to make sure I hadn't left my toothbrush in the bathroom.

"Mom, I see how the man looks at you. It's because of your lifetime of friendship that he can see you for who you are, no matter what happened in those twenty years you were away. And friendship is the best foundation for a romantic relationship."

"That's pretty deep," I said, wondering how we'd gotten to the point where she now gave me relationship advice. Especially considering how angry she'd been with me after her father and I had divorced a couple of years earlier.

Pink tinged Lilly's cheeks as she admitted, "I read it in a magazine."

Or there was that.

"Well, you're not wrong. But just know that it might not end the way you're hoping."

Lilly smiled, like she knew something I didn't. "Maybe." Her smile faltered. "In all seriousness, though, it would be nice to have Benji around on a more permanent basis. You know, considering Dad hasn't been around much lately. He's missed his last few phone calls with us. He didn't used to."

That was what this was about.

I sat down on the edge of the bed and patted next to me, indicating for Lilly to sit. My kids did still need me, and that was a comforting thought.

"Your dad—you know he loves you very much."

Lilly rolled her eyes. "You're supposed to tell me that. But if he loved us so much, why doesn't he make more of an effort? He was trying, right after the divorce. We saw him nearly every weekend. Now..."

"Now, he has a lot more responsibility than he did before. You know he has a new book coming out. There is even more publicity around this one than the last, plus he still has his position as department head at the university."

She nodded, like she'd heard this all before, which she had. "I know, and it's not like he lives in town, but the three-hour drive didn't used to bother him. Now he uses it as an excuse."

"Dad promised he's taking you two on vacation during spring break," I pointed out, praying he wouldn't cancel. Planning anything that far in advance was next to impossible these days.

Lilly stood and gave me a forced smile. "Yes, he did."

I could tell she didn't believe it was actually going to happen, but I returned her smile, as if I did.

A knock on the front door told me that Benji had arrived.

My heart rate spiked, and my palms were suddenly moist.

This was Benji. My best friend. The man with whom I'd spent thousands of hours over the course of my lifetime and would likely spend thousands more.

Nothing to be nervous about.

"Go get 'em, tiger," Lilly said, now wearing a smile that was nothing but genuine.

I wished I could do the same, but I suddenly found myself wanting to hide in the bathroom and never come out.

"Mom, Benji's here," Flash called up the stairs. That meant he'd answered the door and Benji was now inside.

Panic.

For a psychologist, I sure had a lot of unaddressed anxieties.

It wasn't until Lilly picked up my suitcase and pushed me toward the hallway that I managed to start walking.

"It's just for one night," she reminded me. "Two days. And most of the time you'll be involved in wedding activities."

Wedding activities.

I was Benji's plus-one.

That was a best friend kind of thing, right?

When I descended the stairs and saw Benji standing by the door, wearing an old T-shirt and a baseball cap, I relaxed. As the town's handyman, this was Benji's signature look, and it immediately put me at ease. He wasn't a prom date or someone looking to impress.

He then held up the largest bag of chocolate candy I'd ever seen. "I've come prepared," he said with a grin that lit up his eyes.

I laughed, and the anxiety clenching my stomach loosened its grip. Because this was my best friend in the entire world, who knew me better than anyone else.

There would be no kids this weekend and no mothers.

And I couldn't wait to walk out that door and see what White Sands National Park had in store for us.

Something magical, I was sure.

F act: I knew we were going to a wedding.

Fact: I knew that the Garretts had been one of the wealthiest families in Amor.

Fact: Somehow, I was still left speechless when we pulled in front of the fanciest resort I'd ever seen.

It towered over Benji's little car, and a valet stood out front, ready to take our keys. I shared an anxious glance with Benji, he in his faded T-shirt and me in my leggings and tennis shoes. We still had a couple of hours before the wedding, giving us enough time to change, but I suddenly had my doubts that we belonged there.

Or at least that *I* belonged there. My mother, in an attempt to get me to reconsider attending the wedding, had made it very clear that we and the Garretts were cut from different cloth. And that our cloths weren't compatible.

I wondered if that would make a difference this weekend.

"You didn't mention we were staying at such a high-end resort," I said, stepping out of the car.

"I didn't know," Benji said. "I mean, I knew the Garretts had done well. But this... This is more than I was expecting."

Benji's parents had insisted on paying for our rooms because we were going to the wedding on their behalf, and I hated to think how much they had spent. I didn't allow myself to feel guilty, though, because it wouldn't change anything. Only thing to do now was enjoy it.

The valet moved in to take Benji's keys while a bellhop reached for our luggage. Part of me wanted to resist. It felt weird allowing a stranger to do something I was capable of doing myself. And then having to tip them for the unnecessary service.

But before I could find the words, Benji had already given the bellhop our names, and he was loading our suitcases onto a luggage trolley.

"My name is Elijah," the bellhop said, his toothy grin taking up most of his face. His eyes crinkled, bringing his freckled skin to life. He must have sensed my anxiety about letting him take my suitcase because he said, "Don't worry, your luggage is safe with me." And then he released the most amusing laugh I'd ever heard. It was a bit on the squeaky side, like if a mouse had a laughing fit. But it was genuine and immediately put me at ease.

"Hello, Elijah," I said, returning his smile. "I'm not certain what room we're in yet. If you'd rather, we can take our suitcases, so you don't have to be bothered with it."

I hoped he'd take me up on my offer, but no such luck.

Instead, I was once again on the receiving end of Elijah's laughter. "It's my job, and honestly, if I'm not helping you with your luggage, what else am I going to do?"

Right.

"Well, thank you. I appreciate it."

Elijah's grin grew. "You don't know how nice that is to hear. It's a rarity nowadays."

The valet threw an annoyed frown in Elijah's direction, like he felt Elijah was being too talkative—too candid—with the guests.

But I liked it. It wasn't often you met someone who was so real.

Elijah didn't seem to notice his co-worker's annoyance and pointed toward the hotel's front doors. "Straight inside and to the left you'll find reception. You can check in and pick up your room key there."

"Thank you, Elijah," I called after him as he sped away with the luggage trolley. I wondered how he'd know where to take it.

Especially because when we approached the counter, the receptionist didn't seem to be able to find our names.

"It's probably under my mom's name," Benji said, not looking as ruffled as I felt. "Margo Stephens."

Margo. I'd always loved that name. It was so exotic, even though Benji's mother had lived in our small New Mexican town her entire life, never traveling further than the next state over.

"Oh, yes," the receptionist said with a smile, and I relaxed. Nothing to be worried about. Margo had booked the rooms, so it made sense that they would be in her name. "She told us you would be staying with us. I just need to see your IDs."

After checking our driver's licenses, the receptionist handed Benji a small packet that contained a couple of cards and a map. "Your luggage will be waiting for you upstairs. Just let us know if you need anything, and we'll make sure to get you taken care of."

"Thank you."

Benji turned toward the elevator, but when the receptionist didn't hand me the key cards for my room, I asked, "Can I get my keys and map as well?"

The receptionist handed me an additional map, then nodded toward Benji. "The packet contains both of your key cards."

I found that odd, considering every other hotel I'd ever been in gave me key cards for each room separately. But I supposed if the rooms were right next door to each other, it made sense to send the key cards together.

Benji and I rode the elevator up to the ninth floor, deciding that once we'd cleaned up and dressed for the wedding, we'd meet back in the lobby to figure out where we were supposed to go from there.

Except, when I asked Benji what my room number was, he said he didn't know.

"All it says is 927 on the packet of key cards, along with the Wi-Fi password," he said.

I knew it. It wasn't just my anxiety acting up.

Unease set in. This needed to be a "no pressure" kind of weekend. Benji was wearing faded jeans and a baseball cap. He had the beginnings of a beard. That was the very definition of no pressure.

Never mind that he looked amazing in all of it.

"Your mom wouldn't have... What I mean is... She told you she reserved two rooms, didn't she?"

Benji's eyebrows scrunched as he flipped the packet over, looking genuinely perplexed. When he didn't see anything written on the opposite side, his gaze met mine. "She said she'd taken care of our reservation and not to worry about anything. That it was an all-inclusive resort."

Reservation. Singular.

Before I could point this out, realization spread across his features, and Benji pulled his phone out. It couldn't have rung more than once or twice before his mom picked up. "Hey, Mom." A pause. "Yes, it's gorgeous." Another pause. "That's the thing, Mom. We were only given key cards to one room."

I held my breath. It was a mistake. It was all going to be taken care of.

Benji stilled. "I see. You might have mentioned this earlier." He threw a glance my way and gave me a smile, but it was strained, as if he was about to be the bearer of bad news. "Love you too." He slid the phone into his pocket.

"There's only one room," I guessed.

"A suite with two bedrooms, actually," he said. "Apparently it was less expensive than getting the rooms separately. She figured it wouldn't be a big deal, considering we've been inseparable since we were toddlers. You've vacationed with my family in cabins where we both slept in the loft, and she figured this wouldn't be much different."

I turned a smile on Benji, hoping he didn't see my anxiety through it. "All right, let's get settled, then."

It would be fine. No big deal. So what, I'd been having feelings lately that I'd never thought I'd have toward my best friend. And now we were sharing a hotel room.

Of course, calling it a hotel room would have been an insult to the room we walked into. It was larger than I had expected, and the exquisite detail that surrounded me made it feel three times bigger. From the complimentary chocolate truffles that sat on a small dining room table to the hand towels that had been shaped into swans, extensive thought had been given to every aspect of the suite. My suitcase was already waiting for me by one of the king-size beds, and the curtains had been opened, allowing me to see out past our balcony. White Sands National Park sat just beyond the resort golf course, the sand dunes sparkling in the sun.

I was no longer thinking about the awkward sleeping arrangement and instead that I was a bit disappointed we'd only get one night in this place. I doubted I'd ever get the chance again.

A notification chimed on my phone, reminding me that the wedding started in two hours, and I'd need most of that time to shower and make myself decent. After seeing the type of place we were staying at, I was feeling the pressure. Thank goodness Lilly had switched my dresses last minute, or I'd have felt even more under-dressed than I was already going to be.

Benji had disappeared into the other room, where his luggage had been waiting for him, and I called over to him. "You okay if I jump in the shower?"

"Ladies first," he called back. "Besides, I know how long you take."

Yes, he did. Benji knew me better than even my own mother. We'd been friends too long, experienced too much, for it to be any different.

And that thought was comforting.

This wasn't any different from when we had been teenagers. Just a new location.

I relaxed and smiled.

Of course, Benji had been right about how long I'd take. The water pressure in the massive walk-in shower was amazing, and I lost track of time, enjoying my first shower in years where I didn't have someone knocking on the door, asking if I was about done.

Unfortunately, that lack of reminder also meant that by the time I jumped out, I only had thirty minutes to finish getting ready, and Benji hadn't even had the chance to use it. I hadn't needed to worry about him, though, because by the time I had returned with my dress on, he was already finished with his shower.

"I didn't want to take long because I knew you'd need the bathroom to finish getting fancy," he told me with a smirk, disappearing into his room.

I tried to ignore what that smirk did to me.

And then I realized his beard was gone. I hadn't seen him clean-shaven since before I'd left Amor two decades earlier. A wave of memories crashed over me.

"You shaved," I called after him. I didn't know why I felt the need to state the obvious, but it was rather shocking.

Benji poked his head back out. "You sound disappointed." His eyes seemed to be laughing at me—teasing me.

"Just surprised is all."

Benji disappeared back into his room. "We're fancy now, remember?" he called. "Gotta represent my parents well."

I supposed he was right.

Twenty minutes later, Benji entered the expansive bathroom. I was only halfway finished curling my hair, but at least my makeup was done. His eyes widened a fraction. "Dang, you look amazing."

Heat rushed into my cheeks. "Thank you." I glanced at my phone. "I know we're supposed to be heading down now. I'm almost done. Promise."

Benji raised a skeptical eyebrow. "Why don't I go figure out where the wedding is, and you can meet me there?"

I was grateful for his understanding. It wasn't often I dressed up beyond my work attire, so I wasn't as proficient in the art of hair and makeup.

It took some superhuman abilities, but I was only ten minutes behind schedule when I grabbed my purse from the bed and rushed out of the room. Twenty minutes until the wedding.

Benji had sent me a text asking me to meet him at the front desk and said that he knew where we needed to go. I bounced on my toes, willing the elevator to move faster.

When the doors finally opened, I didn't bother checking which floor I was on, assuming it was the lobby. A tall, good-looking man moved around me and into the elevator as I stepped out. A scowl twisted his handsome features as he threw a parting glance down the hallway. By the time I realized I'd only made it to the fifth floor, the elevator doors had shut, and I found myself having to wait for the next one.

"You here for the wedding?" someone behind me asked.

I turned, startled, because I'd sworn I was by myself. But three doors down, a man sat on the floor, his back against the wall. He wore a tuxedo but otherwise had the look of a disheveled vagabond, his hair standing on end and a couple days' worth of growth on his chin.

"I am." I pressed the elevator button several times in quick succession, like that would make it come faster.

"Me too," the man said. "You want to know the worst part of weddings? Aside from my family and my fiancée, I don't know a single person here." He paused. "I suppose that's not completely true. Most of my father's business associates have graced us with their presence, and I've been working on making some connections there. But take you, for example. I don't know you. We've never met. And yet I have to pretend to be glad to see you."

That gave me pause, and I stepped away from the elevator, curious. "You're the groom?"

The man laughed, though it lacked humor. "See? You don't know me either. But now you're going to feel obligated to tell me congratulations and how happy you are to be here." He looked me over, as if trying to figure out what my connection to the wedding was. "Are you the wife of one of my dad's business associates? You seem too young, but you never know with that lot."

It had been a long time since someone had accused me of being too young, and heat rushed into my cheeks. "No, I'm not. My friend's parents are friends with your fiancée's parents."

The groom laughed again, but this time he really did seem amused. "That's even worse. So, you don't even know Bree?"

I hesitated, then shook my head.

He laughed again and pushed himself up to a standing position before sticking out his hand. "I'm Mark."

"Hi, Mark." I took his hand and shook it, but quickly pulled back. His grip was cold, and firm. He was used to getting what he wanted, when he wanted it.

"What do you say you come in and take a load off? We can get to know each other a little better." He took a step toward me. "Must be hard not knowing anyone here." The smell of alcohol radiated off him. Hopefully he wouldn't come in contact with open flames, because he would set off a small explosion.

I took a step back. "I'm actually meeting my friend down in the lobby, but thank you for the offer."

"Oh, yes. The friend whose parents know Bree's parents." Mark took another step toward me. "You're just here for the free food and alcohol, then. That's what weddings are all about, aren't they? That, and finding a single man who is here for the same thing. It's the ultimate breeding grounds. No one cares about the bride and groom. Not really. Their happiness—it's inconsequential."

What was going on here? I took another step back.

"Shouldn't you be headed down to your wedding? You'll be getting married in fifteen minutes—I'm sure everyone is worried about you."

He waved a hand through the air. "Been postponed by a couple of hours. Something to do with the minister having car problems."

I hesitated, my inner therapist kicking in. "So, you decided to spend it sitting in the hallway, getting drunk and hitting on random women who happen to walk by? That doesn't sound like you want to get married. Maybe the wedding getting postponed is a sign."

Mark snorted. "What, like a sign from the universe?" He gave a quick shake of his head. "No, the universe and I aren't on speaking terms. Much like my fiancée and me. So, yes, I'm sitting in a hallway, drunk, hitting on random women. Because if someone were to actually say yes, it would be the only good thing I could expect from today."

I no longer saw a creepy and loveless groom but a broken man who desperately needed help. "Cheating on Bree isn't going to fix whatever issues you and she are going through. Maybe she's the one you need to be with right now."

Just the mention of Bree seemed to trigger something in Mark. His features twisted, and his anger made him nearly unrecognizable. When I looked into his eyes, there was no love there. "No. I don't think that would be wise."

This man was broken far beyond what an hour-long therapy session could fix. Beyond what a lifetime of therapy sessions could fix, even.

I always made a point of not making assumptions about those who walked into my therapy office, and I attempted to apply those principles now. But the way this man held himself—the wild look in his eyes, as if he was capable of doing anything—I was afraid.

As if on cue, the elevator dinged behind me and the doors opened.

"I hope you figure things out," I said, backing up and into the elevator. "I really do. And just in case you decide to go through with the wedding, I'll see you in two hours." Mark took a step toward me, and I punched the CLOSE button. Just before the doors shut, I called out, "Oh, and congratulations!"

As the elevator began moving, I blew out a hard breath and leaned against the wall.

Well, this was a fun way to start the weekend.

4

When I walked into the lobby downstairs, my gaze immediately sought out Benji. I wished I'd have been able to get ready faster. If I had, Benji would have been with me when I came downstairs. I wouldn't have been feeling rushed, I wouldn't have gotten off on the wrong floor, and that encounter with Mark would never have happened.

I found Benji talking with the receptionist and, after throwing a paranoid look over my shoulder toward the elevators, I made a beeline for him. I doubted Mark had followed me—it would have been too much effort for someone who was looking for the easiest way to distract himself from the fact that he was getting married in two hours—but, just in case, I wanted Benji by my side.

"Hey, there you are," Benji said, turning to me with a smile. "I was just about to call you. I was getting information on what is available at the resort. Gotta make the most of our time here this weekend."

"I know I took forever. Sorry." I threw another glance toward the elevators before returning Benji's smile. I hoped it didn't look strained. "I ran into Mark, Bree's fiancé, on the way down, and it turns out the wedding has been postponed by a couple of hours."

The receptionist looked surprised. "That's strange. No one passed the message on to me." She scribbled something onto a piece of paper. "I guess the groom would know best, though."

"We have two hours to relax, then." Benji walked over to some oversized chairs in the lobby and collapsed into one of them. He looked tired, and we'd only just arrived. Then again, he'd been the one to drive.

"I suppose the pool is out of the question," I said, imagining us sunbathing in our dress and suit. I sat on a straight-back chair next to him.

"And we probably shouldn't eat, considering they'll have food at the reception. That, and I know I'll spill my lunch all over me." Benji closed his eyes and settled deeper into his chair. "We definitely need to go sledding on the sand dunes before we leave, though."

"We could always just walk the grounds and explore a bit."

"We could. But a nap also sounds good," Benji murmured, eyes still closed, sounding half-asleep.

I laughed and stood, then stuck out a hand to help

Benji up. "You look exhausted. It took me long enough to get ready, though, that I'm not going to undo it all by lying in bed. Why don't you sleep, and I'll call the kids—see how they're doing."

Benji took my hand and pulled himself to his feet.

We stood closer than should have been comfortable, but neither of us moved right away, him still holding my hand. Or was it the other way around?

"I—" My voice stuck in my throat.

I what? Before I could figure it out, Benji had let go and taken a step back.

"All right, you got yourself a deal," he said with a crooked smile. "Thank goodness for late weddings. I'm so tired, I'm just hoping I wake back up."

I folded my arms across my chest, not knowing what else to do with my hands since Benji had let go.

"Don't worry, I won't let you miss the wedding. You know, considering you're the one who dragged me here for it."

Benji slung an arm around my shoulders in the familiar way he always had. "Women love weddings, though. You'll do anything for the chance to get all dressed up."

I scrunched up my nose. "Do you know anything about women? The best thing about weddings is the food. It's always about the food."

Mark had been right about that part.

I slipped out from under Benji's arm and pressed the UP button on the elevator.

"Well, whether you like dressing up or not, you do it well," Benji said, tossing a lopsided smile my way. He paused. "That sounded weird. What I meant was that you look nice. I like your dress. And your hair." He shook his head, pink tinging his cheeks. "You know what I mean."

I had to hold in a smile. He was adorable when he got all flustered. "Yes, I do. And thank you for the compliment."

"Mind if I walk you to your room?" he asked as we exited onto the ninth floor. His tone held a teasing lilt.

"Only if it's not too much trouble," I said with a laugh. But when we reached our door, I hesitated. "You know, I'm actually going to go downstairs to call the kids."

Benji inserted the key card and opened the door. "You can always do it from your room in here. It wouldn't bother me."

Maybe not. But I was feeling antsy and needed to get some fresh air. I didn't know if it was because of Benji, the wedding, or being away from the kids, but anxiety, my constant companion, had settled in my gut, and I needed to walk it off.

"Thanks, but I think I'll call them outside."

Benji nodded and lifted one hand in a tired wave. "Tell the kids hi for me."

My mind jumped to what Lilly had told me, right before Benji had picked me up. How she hoped that he would become a more permanent part of our lives in the future.

The anxiety in my gut doubled.

"Will do," I told him, then hurried away. Because I was as transparent as they come, and I didn't want Benji to see the war that raged inside me.

The one that told me that Benji was my forever person. And always had been.

And how much that terrified me.

WHEN I CALLED to check in on the kids, Flash was in the middle of a computer hacking competition, so Lilly yelled at him that "Mom says hi," then proceeded to tell me that their grandmother had canceled Trish's lunch order from the diner because she thought the kids ate out too often and they needed a home-cooked meal. Never mind that Trish had already lived in Amor for nearly two years as my and the kids' roommate, and she and I took turns cooking throughout the week. My mother still thought of her as the newcomer—the outsider.

"I bet that didn't go over well," I said, knowing Trish would have thought of ordering out as a special treat while I was gone. I allowed my feet to take me where they wanted, which ended up being out the double doors by the golf shop.

"Trish stormed up to her room and refuses to come

back down as long as Grandma is here. Grandma says that's fine by her, more food for the rest of us."

Oh, dear. Maybe I should have just assumed everything was going well and not called.

"You tell Trish that I'm going to make a giant key lime pie for her when I get home. And there will be ice cream to go with it."

Lilly laughed, but then said, "In all seriousness, you'll need the pie, ice cream, and a full tray of brownies. At least. Want me to hand over the phone so you can tell her yourself?"

I cringed. "I would, but I have a wedding I have to go to." Guilt gnawed at me as I told Lilly to pass my love on to everyone, then hung up before I could hear any more about how awful things were going back home.

After slipping the phone into my purse, I realized I had no idea where I was. Stopping, I took a moment to look around and saw that I was on a path that wound its way through the resort grounds, but my view of anything worth seeing was blocked by the tall hotel. I pulled in a long breath as I continued my walk, letting the ambiance of the resort wash over me while trying to rid myself of the guilt of leaving my kids for the weekend.

A luxury swimming pool appeared on my right, and it looked so enticing that, for a split second, I was tempted to skip the wedding and spend the afternoon there instead. Palm trees surrounded the water, colorful cabanas with tables and reclining chairs dotted the landscape, and servers walked around carrying large trays of food.

That was my kind of pool.

I forced myself to shun the thought as soon as it appeared. Our presence here was important enough to Benji's parents that they had paid for our room at this beautiful resort, and the least we could do was represent them well.

Even if the groom was a terrible person, and the soon-to-be newlyweds weren't on speaking terms.

Who was I to judge?

I rounded a corner on the path. If I kept going, I'd end up on the golf course. In the distance I saw the bellhop from earlier driving a golf cart to the opposite side, tossing a large smile to anyone he passed. I waved, but he didn't notice me. Not wanting to be pelted by stray golf balls, I turned on a different path.

One that led me straight to a wedding.

Looked like they had been able to fill in the vacant time slot with no problem.

Except, that didn't make sense, considering the last-minute change. Even the receptionist hadn't known the wedding had been delayed.

And the closer I got, the more I realized that something with this wedding had gone terribly wrong. Half the guests were leaving, and the other half were arguing. From what I could tell, there was no bride or groom present.

An older gentleman hurried up to me as I was

passing a table filled with presents and a tall wedding cake. The cake knife sat precariously on the edge of the table, and I pushed it back before it could fall on the ground.

"Please accept our apologies," the man said, out of breath and looking a bit worse for wear. "I hope we can still count on your business."

I took a step back. "I'm sorry, but I'm not who you think I am."

The man eyed my dress and my curled hair. "You aren't here for the wedding?"

"I am here for a wedding, but mine was delayed by a couple of hours."

The man's lips parted in surprise. "Oh, dear. I see that you met Mark. Yes, he was under the impression it had been delayed. Only...well...it wasn't. And now it appears there won't be a wedding at all." He hesitated. "So, you're sure we don't do business with you?"

I gave him a reassuring smile. "No. I am here with Benji Stephens, in lieu of Margo and Dean Stephens. They were devastated that they couldn't make it themselves."

At the mention of Benji's parents, the man's expression brightened. "Benji is here? Margo and Dean are some of the best people in the world. I told them they didn't need to feel guilty about not being here, but they insisted on at least Benji representing them."

"You must be Mr. Garrett, then," I said, realization settling in. This man was Melinda and Bree's father, and not at all what I had been expecting. "I'm Maddie Swallows, Laurie Dawson's daughter."

To my surprise, considering my mother's assertions that she'd been in a feud with the Garretts for the past thirty years, Mr. Garrett's expression brightened even more. "Maddie, I remember when you were a little girl. Is your mother still keeping things lively in Amor? I always loved when she was at the town meetings. Kept it entertaining."

That was one way to put it. At least he recalled those meetings with fondness, unlike others in town.

"If I may ask, why has the wedding been canceled?"

Mr. Garrett now looked uncomfortable, his smile dipping. "Well, let's say there has been a series of unfortunate events. Not the least of which was the fact that Bree and Mark were completely wrong for each other from the start. I'm sorry you came all this way for nothing." A pause. "I suppose someone should tell the groom, shouldn't they?"

I started. "You mean, he doesn't know?"

Mr. Garrett's expression of discomfort morphed into guilt. "I'm afraid that Mark and Bree's delayed wedding was a ruse to buy us some time. I'm unsure where Bree is at the moment. Probably packing."

I couldn't help my sigh of relief. After meeting Mark, I thought that even if Bree was anything like Melinda, no one deserved to enter a marriage like that.

Mr. Garrett studied me for a moment, his expression quizzical. "You look happy about that."

It was my turn to feel guilty. I raised a shoulder. "From what little interaction I've had with Mark, I think Bree is probably better off."

"I always knew I liked you," Mr Garrett said, his smile returning. Someone called his name and he briefly glanced over his shoulder. "Hopefully you'll still manage to enjoy your weekend."

I thought of Benji back up in our room. "I think I will."

Mr. Garrett gave me an apologetic smile when his name was repeated. "Looks like I'm needed elsewhere." And then he hurried away as I surveyed the wreckage.

A middle-aged woman was sitting on the front row of seats, alternating between sobbing and yelling at a man who looked to be her husband. The only words I could make out were, "Why isn't he here?" Over and over again.

Those must have been Mark's parents. Mark's father sent Mr. Garrett what seemed to be an exasperated look. From all appearances, he didn't seem at all upset and, unless I was mistaken, he looked like he didn't think any more of the wedding than Mr. Garrett had. That was interesting.

A woman who looked vaguely familiar was running around with a forced smile, talking to people, seemingly attempting to calm things down.

Mrs. Garrett.

The poor woman looked frazzled as she tried to do damage control.

Interestingly enough, I didn't see any bridesmaids or groomsmen. Now that I was really looking, there weren't any young people at all. Not even Melinda was there. Just a bunch of disgruntled-looking old people.

Scratch that. A guy who looked to be in his twenties stood at the back of the venue with a frowning redheaded woman in a gorgeous floor-length jade dress. She was shaking her head, then abruptly turned and stormed off.

I released a heavy breath.

This was some wedding.

5

I knew weddings were bittersweet and there was usually some crying, but this was more than I could handle. You'd think that as a psychologist, I'd be a pro at dealing with intense emotion, but it was quite the opposite. It always put me on edge. Maybe that was what actually made me a good therapist—I did everything in my power to replace all of that with a calm reassurance that my clients could work through whatever life was throwing at them. Without the drama.

When I finally managed to escape and return to our suite, Benji was just coming out of his room. He'd slept in his suit, so it was wrinkled, and his hair stood up on end. "What time is it?" he asked.

I bit back a laugh. Even when the man was disheveled and looking lost, he was adorable.

"Time for us to eat. I'm starving. And then I'm taking you sledding."

Benji blinked twice. Then again. Like he was attempting to process my words. "But...the wedding. It's starting soon."

The image of all those arguing people jumped to the front of my mind, and I released a long sigh. "No. It isn't. It was never delayed. It was canceled."

He looked down at his wrinkled suit. "But I dressed fancy. I never dress fancy. I even shaved."

Truer words had never been spoken. And as nice as he looked right now, I missed his scruff.

"I know, but trust me, it's for the best. I talked with Mr. Garrett, and they only told Mark it had been delayed to buy themselves some time. Apparently, Mark isn't the type to just accept things, like the fact that his fiancée didn't love him."

Benji looked forlornly down at his suit again. "But I dressed fancy."

I laughed and walked toward him, then used my hand to smooth down his hair. "Yes, so I saw. Let's change and go down to get some dinner, huh? It will help you feel better."

And maybe it would help him forget the fact that he'd have to wait a few days for his stubble to grow back in. Benji wasn't a hairy guy, and the fact that he could even attempt to grow a beard was a feat in itself.

"Food does seem to have that effect," he said, turning back to his room. Benji hadn't taken more than a couple of steps when he looked back over his shoulder. "Oh, and just because we're staying somewhere fancy doesn't mean we have to eat fancy. Nothing I can't pronounce, okay?"

"You have my word."

I watched as Benji returned to his room, my feelings for that adorably awkward man exploding, and I attempted to shove them back down.

It was near impossible, though, considering we were at a beautiful resort and there was no longer anything to distract us from the fact that we were here together. Alone. No wedding. No need for me to act as bodyguard against all the single ladies who would no doubt have fallen for Benji's small-town charm.

Just him and me.

"I CAN'T BELIEVE they rent sleds out of the golf shop," Benji said, using his sled as a cane as we trekked across the golf course. "There were more people renting sleds than clubs."

"Makes sense," I said, placing my sled on top of my head and seeing if I could get it to balance. "It's why people come to White Sands National Park. Sure, it's the largest gypsum dunefield in the world and can actually be seen from space. But that's only an interesting fact. This"—I pointed to the sled on my head— "is why people come. So they can sled in shorts and T-shirts. The sand never gets hot, and they don't have to get wet and cold from snow. Win-win."

Benji tossed me a smile. "And it's the only reason you agreed to come to this wedding with me."

"That's...only partially true," I said with a grin.

The conversation stalled as I followed him along a paved path that left the resort and headed into the dunes. It wasn't awkward silence, though, and Benji seemed perfectly content pushing ahead and enjoying the view. The white sand might have looked like snow, but it didn't act like it, each step a chore as we left the path and worked our way to the top of the tallest dune in the vicinity.

"Admit it," Benji said, his breaths coming fast as we reached the summit. "You're relieved the wedding was canceled so that we can do stuff like this, rather than spending the day with all those rich tech people."

"I'll admit that I'm glad to not have to pretend I belong in that environment, and grateful that Bree didn't end up with Mark. But the end of any relationship is difficult, even if it wasn't a healthy one."

I collapsed in the sand, my sled next to me. It had been a while since I'd been to White Sands, and I hadn't remembered it being so exhausting. Either the dunes had gotten higher or I had gotten old and out of shape.

Had to be the dunes.

"Of course, for someone who went through a high school girlfriend every two weeks, I suppose there are exceptions," I said, looking up at Benji and waggling my eyebrows.

But rather than give me a mocking smile in return or

push me down the dune as he would have when we were in high school, Benji looked away, a sad frown pulling on his lips.

"I've never known you to take a relationship seriously, that's all," I said, trying to backpedal but failing miserably.

Benji blew out a puff of air. "You're right. I never took it seriously. But after you left, I changed."

Not this again. I understood that I'd hurt him when I'd moved away from Amor. But every time we started to grow close, like we'd been before, he used it to push me away.

"Yes, and I've apologized dozens of times for that."

Benji looked surprised by my defensive tone. "I didn't mean it as a bad thing. I'm grateful you left. It allowed for us to grow into the people we were meant to be."

That was something he hadn't told me before. And frankly, it kind of stung.

"And with that," he continued, lowering himself onto the sand next to me, "it allowed me to be more honest with what I wanted. That was when I met Candace. We dated for three years before getting engaged. So, trust me when I say that you aren't the only one who understands the pain that comes from the end of a long-term relationship."

Benji had been engaged? The jealousy that accosted me took me by surprise. I had been married and had the two best kids in the world. I didn't regret a thing.

But the thought of Benji with someone else... It made my stomach churn.

I knew it was a double standard, but that didn't make the jealousy any less intense.

"You never walked down the aisle?" I asked, hoping he couldn't hear how the question choked me up.

He gave a quick shake of his head. "Nope. She got sick five months before the big day. And she never got better."

So, not only had he lost his fiancée, but neither of them had chosen to end the relationship. It had been taken from him.

I'd never been on this side of things before.

When I advised clients who'd lost loved ones, I always told them that they didn't need to feel guilty about moving on. That the new person in their lives wasn't a replacement, and that they shouldn't compare them. It was merely a new chapter.

But I suddenly saw myself as Benji must see me. The one who wasn't Candace. The one who would never be her.

Why hadn't he ever told me about her? Why hadn't my mother? Or anyone else in town, for that matter?

"I'm so sorry," I said, my voice barely above a whisper.

He nudged me with his shoulder, a familiar gesture that could always make me smile, even now. "Don't be. It was an important part of my life, and I'm grateful for it. Just like I'm grateful that you came back into my life. Now, I get to be a better version of myself. For you."

Benji's gaze was so sincere. And intense.

Oh.

"I thought... I mean, I hoped that was the direction we've been moving in. But the best friend barrier—it's been a tough one to cross," I said, my gaze dropping to my lap. "And one that I haven't been sure we'd ever make it over. We both have histories and baggage and—"

Benji leaned forward like he was going to stop my words with a kiss.

Just the subtle movement caused my lips to clamp shut, my eyes to widen, and me to lose my balance—despite the fact that I was sitting down. My hand shot out, and I planted it in the sand behind me.

Except, it didn't feel like sand.

I screeched and shot up into the air, wiping my hand viciously against my pants.

Pain flashed across Benji's features, and I realized what it must have seemed like—like the thought of him kissing me was enough to send me screaming.

And to be fair, it was. If Benji had kissed me, I had no doubt that later that day I'd have screamed in happiness. And panic. And relief. And fear.

But that wasn't what had sent me scrambling.

"There's something under the sand," I said, my voice shaking. "Something hairy. Dead coyote maybe?"

Benji's forehead smoothed, and he chuckled. "I don't think coyotes hang out at the sand dunes, considering they wouldn't have a food source. Are you sure it wasn't your jacket?"

I pointed to my jacket that lay a yard away in the opposite direction. "Not my jacket."

Benji looked like he still thought I was being ridiculous, but he humored me by leaning forward and sticking his hand in the sand. And then he yanked his hand out of the sand so fast, he stumbled backwards.

I thought he might be messing with me, but one glance at him told me he was completely freaked out.

Something was buried in the sand.

"Well, we can't just let an animal rot there," I said. "There's probably someone at the visitor center who can help us take care of it."

Benji nodded slowly. The man climbed into all sorts of dark, creepy places for his job as a handyman, laid traps for all kinds of animals, and had killed more rattlesnakes and scorpions than I could keep track of.

But whatever lay dead in the sand had him unnerved.

When I looked back to the spot where the creature lay, I saw why.

The creature was no longer hidden, our movements having partially unearthed it.

And it wasn't an animal.

Staring up at me was the face of Bree's ex-fiancé.

Mark Peters was dead.

6

I'd seen dead bodies before. I didn't like them any more than the next person, but they weren't completely foreign to me.

That didn't seem to matter when my fight or flight instincts kicked in. Without another thought, I jumped on my sled and slid down that dune faster than I'd thought possible on that little plastic disk.

Benji, on the other hand, managed to keep his wits about him. By the time I'd reached the bottom and looked up, he had stuck his sled in the sand as a marker and was walking back down the dune.

I should have thought of that. Otherwise, with so many miles of dunes, we'd never be able to find the body again.

Which the killer must have been counting on. Too much sand. Too much wide-open space.

Of course, Mark might not have been murdered.

Maybe he came out to the dunes for a walk and just happened to die of natural causes. And then his entire body had been buried in sand. Somehow.

As soon as Benji joined me at the bottom of the dune, I blurted out, "He was murdered. There is a murderer at the resort. Everywhere I go, people drop like flies. Is it my perfume? My aura? In fact, it would be safer if you took me home and I locked myself in my room."

I knew I was being ridiculous. But before I'd moved back to Amor, people hadn't died. Now...bodies were everywhere.

Benji rested a hand on my shoulder in an attempt to calm me down. "This isn't your fault. Let's just focus on contacting the authorities, all right?"

I was in full panic mode, and even Benji's calming presence wasn't enough. "Who do we tell? Is it the resort's security we should contact, or do we need to walk to the White Sands visitor center? I don't even know how long of a walk that is, and it's starting to get dark. What if we get lost or it's closed by the time we get there?"

Benji didn't say anything, instead pulling me into a tight hug. He knew there was no reasoning with me when I got like this. So he held me, letting me know that he was there with me. That I wasn't alone.

And that was enough.

I sucked in a long breath. "You're right. We shouldn't go wandering around. Let's call the police, then head back to our room and not come out until we leave tomorrow."

If only it had been that easy.

We did call the police, and they asked us to stay put until they arrived. Thanks to Benji's sled, we were able to easily show them where we'd found the body, despite the impending darkness.

But then the detective arrived on the scene. He was a man with a thin face and high cheekbones who looked eerily like a skeleton in the glow of the moon.

"You Maddie Swallows and Benji Stephens?" The detective took out a notepad, seemingly ready to record our every word.

I gave a little nod. "Yes, sir."

"I'm Detective Holbrook. You two discovered the body about an hour ago, is that right?"

Discovered the body.

The words sent a chill through me, and I couldn't bring myself to answer the detective. Had it really only been a few short hours ago that I had been backing away from Mark into the elevator?

"Yes, sir." It was Benji who answered this time. He took my hand and gave it a squeeze.

The detective paused and glanced up to the top of the dune, where a photographer had finished taking pictures and two men were now loading the body onto a stretcher.

I looked away.

The detective noticed the action and studied me for a moment longer than necessary. "You've never seen a dead body before." It was a statement, not a question, and he didn't know how wrong he was.

"I have, but it never gets easier," I said.

Detective Holbrook raised an eyebrow. "So, you've seen a lot of dead bodies, then."

I was unsure what the correct answer to that was. The truth didn't seem like the way to go.

Thankfully, Benji came to my rescue. "A woman in our hometown passed away a couple of years ago. It was quite a shock to the community."

He didn't mention that she'd been poisoned or that we'd witnessed another murder last year at a hot air balloon festival. The detective didn't need all those details.

Detective Holbrook scribbled in his notebook. "You staying at the resort?"

"We are," I said, my voice stronger, as if to prove that I could handle the fact that as we were talking, a dead man was being walked past us, like this was normal.

"How long you been there?" he asked.

"Arrived today. Leaving tomorrow."

The detective paused. "Short trip. Anniversary?"

Heat spread into my cheeks, though he'd made an honest mistake. Going away to a fancy resort certainly implied an anniversary trip.

"No," Benji said, too quickly for my liking. "Wedding. Except, it was canceled."

Detective Holbrook lowered his notepad this time, no longer writing. I was unsure why, but the action made me more nervous than when he'd been recording everything we'd been saying. "You were here for Mark Peters' wedding."

Benji threw a questioning look my way, then answered slowly. "Yes. And his fiancée, Bree."

"The same Mark Peters that was reported missing a couple of hours ago. And the same Mark who has just been carried past us." The detective's gaze bore into us, and I was both desperate to know what was going on in that mind of his and terrified.

Even in the limited light, the sun now all but gone, I saw Benji's complexion pale. "That—that was Mark?"

In my panic, I'd forgotten that Benji hadn't met Mark, that he hadn't realized who we'd stumbled upon.

"You've never met the deceased?" the detective asked, his tone skeptical.

Benji shook his head. "We're friends of the bride."

The disappearance of the sun had taken the warmth of the day, and a shiver moved through me.

"Is it all right if we head back to the resort?" I asked, wrapping my arms around my waist. "We didn't see anything that could be of help."

"I'll be the judge of that," the detective said, his gaze boring into me.

Another shiver. This one wasn't from the cold.

"Please?" My voice was timid, and I hated it. But it did the trick.

Detective Holbrook hesitated but then nodded. "Leave

your information with the officer there by the ambulance. Your names, phone numbers, room number at the resort— that kind of thing. We may need to be in touch with further questions."

As we turned to leave, the detective added, "Oh, and you'll need to reserve another night at the resort. We're asking those involved with the wedding to stay put until we've had a chance to talk with everyone. As you can imagine, that will take some time."

"Looks like this little vacation has just been extended," Benji said, releasing a long breath. He didn't sound thrilled by the prospect. But then he tossed a faint smile in my direction. "Not that I don't want to spend more time with you."

I knew the feeling. I was going to have to call Trish and let her know I wouldn't be in the office on Monday. And that she was going to have to deal with my mother on her own a little longer.

"We'll just have to make the best of it," I said, pumping as much excitement into my words as possible. "But maybe no sledding for a while."

7

I didn't know why I'd actually expected that Benji and I could spend the remainder of the weekend quietly enjoying each other's company. I'd thought that maybe we'd even figure out what had been on the other side of that kiss he'd nearly given me.

That was before the knock on our door at eight-thirty the next morning.

It was too early for housekeeping, and we hadn't requested a wakeup call. That left one other possibility, which was why I wasn't at all surprised to discover Detective Holbrook standing on the other side of our door.

"Good morning, Detective," I said, attempting to blink the sleep from my eyes. "You're up early."

The detective harrumphed. "Never went to sleep." Now that I examined him a little closer in the light of day rather than by the moonlight of the previous evening, he did look as if he could use some rest. His eyes were bloodshot, and the bags under his eyes were big enough to use as pillows.

"Benji is still in his room, but you're more than welcome to take a nap on the couch," I said as I opened the door wider. I was mostly kidding, but the man really did look like if he didn't sit down, he'd fall over.

Detective Holbrook ignored me. "What was your relationship with Mark Peters?"

Guess we were getting down to business. But I was unsure why the detective thought I had a relationship with Mark.

I gave him a blank stare.

"What was your relationship with him?" Detective Holbrook repeated.

Benji exited his room at that moment, looking like we'd woken him, and interjected. "What was her relationship with who?"

"Mark Peters." The detective's tone held impatience, like questioning me hadn't been a chore he'd chosen for himself and he'd rather get on with his day.

Benji tossed me a quizzical look before his gaze returned to Detective Holbrook. "She doesn't know this Mark guy. Only came along to the wedding because I invited her."

The detective studied Benji, his expression skeptical.

"I don't," I insisted, finally finding my voice. "I met him once when I got off the elevator on the wrong floor. And that's it."

Detective Holbrook pulled out his trusty notebook and scribbled something in it. "So, you knew which floor he was staying on."

"No, I told you, I got off on the wrong floor."

Detective Holbrook's pen paused, and he glanced up at me. "That was an awfully long conversation for not knowing the man."

"How do you know the length of my conversation?"

Detective Holbrook pointed up at the ceiling in the hallway. "Security cameras."

Right. Of course they'd have looked at those. I hadn't wanted to get into what had happened with the late groom, but it looked like there would be no getting around it. Maybe I could leave out the more embarrassing details. Like how he'd invited me into his room to "get to know each other a little better."

"He looked sad—as if he wasn't doing too well," I said, "and I thought maybe I could help."

"Maddie is a psychologist," Benji told the detective, as if that explained everything. "She owns her own therapy office."

Detective Holbrook studied me for a moment longer. "I see." He slipped the notebook back into his pocket and straightened. "All the same, I'll need you to come downstairs to the security office for some additional questioning. I'll also need your fingerprints."

I blinked rapidly, trying to understand what this detective was telling me. "You want me to take the time to go down to the security office and be interrogated—on my first vacation away from my kids—because I talked to a guy in a hotel hallway?"

"No," the detective said, motioning for me to follow him. "I want you to come with me because you are the last person to see Mark Peters. Both alive and dead."

"I SWEAR I didn't do it," I told Benji as we waited in the security office. Detective Holbrook had already taken my digital fingerprints, and we had been told he'd be with us in a moment.

That had been a lot of moments ago.

"Of course you didn't," Benji said with a small laugh. "I'm sure there's been a mistake and the detective is on his way here right now to apologize."

Benji was the type of man I needed in my life. The kind that laughed at the thought of me being guilty of murder. That thought me incapable of it. Every woman needed that kind of guy.

Detective Holbrook was not that man.

He strode in and didn't bother sitting down, instead leaning against the wall and looking straight at me. "I need to speak with you. Alone."

That wasn't good. I knew the police liked to interrogate people separately so they couldn't coordinate their stories, which meant that I wasn't yet off the hook.

Benji gave me a wary glance, and I squeezed his hand

and smiled in return, letting him know I'd be fine. I didn't let on that my insides were shriveling and I was freaking out.

Never mind that I knew I was innocent. The previous year, I'd had to do everything in my power to prove an innocent man hadn't done the same thing I was being accused of. Murder.

Last year, we'd gotten lucky.

Now, I wasn't so sure.

Benji stood slowly, pushing his chair back. I could tell he didn't want to leave me, but he rested a reassuring hand on my shoulder and then slipped outside.

Alone. I didn't like this.

"Don't worry, we'll be questioning him next," the detective said.

That didn't make me feel any better.

"I don't understand how Mark can be dead," I said. "And how I could be the last one to have seen him alive. After he and I spoke, it was hours until we found the body."

Detective Holbrook consulted a pad of paper that sat next to him on the desk. "Yes, four hours and twenty-seven minutes, to be exact."

"And not a single other person walked down that hallway for the next four hours?"

The detective was quiet long enough to make me feel uncomfortable, which I was sure was his plan.

"Five minutes after you left, Mark went back to his

room. And never left again. No one else entered. And then he winds up dead, with your fingerprints on the murder weapon."

My calm composure was all but gone as I gasped. "What?" I grasped wildly for an explanation, then realized I had no idea what the murder weapon even was. "How did I supposedly kill the guy?"

The detective studied me, maybe trying to ascertain whether I really didn't know. "The cake knife from his own failed wedding. Blood was wiped off, but we still found traces. From the looks of things, he was killed maybe an hour after you had left him. Could be less. His body was moved to the dunes after he was dead."

I had seen that knife—it had been hastily thrown onto the cake table at the wedding, and I'd had to straighten it. But why would it have been used to murder someone? Other weapons would have been much more convenient, and less visible. Maybe that was why it had been used.

"You look like you don't believe me." The detective didn't sound angry but curious why I didn't think it possible the groom could be killed with the knife.

"It's not that I don't believe you." My words came out slowly as I tried to make sense of the situation. "Only, I don't see how any of this scenario could have happened the way you say it did."

Okay, that was another way of saying I didn't believe him.

The detective finally made his way to his own chair

and sat down. He leaned back, his fingers steepled under his chin. "Go on."

"When I left Mark, he was drunk, and from what little interaction I had with him, I'm not surprised someone wanted him dead."

The detective raised an eyebrow. Not the best start, I could admit.

"But," I continued, "he was under the impression that the wedding had been postponed. It hadn't been true, of course, just a way to buy time until the wedding could be canceled. But that's the point. No one else had been told the same message, so everyone else who knew Mark was down at the wedding."

"Where the cake knife was. You're telling me that everyone at that wedding had access to the murder weapon."

I hadn't thought of it that way. "Well, yes, I suppose they did. But when I finally arrived, the place was beginning to clear out, and the cake knife was still there. It had been placed precariously at the edge of the table, and I moved it so it wouldn't fall."

The detective gave a thoughtful nod. "Go on."

"All I'm saying is that I couldn't have killed Mark. For one, I never returned to the fifth floor. In fact, I didn't return to the hotel at all for quite some time, instead choosing to explore the grounds for a bit because Benji was sleeping up in our room. Figured I'd give him a little more time, since we no longer had a wedding to attend."

The detective straightened, like something I'd said was interesting to him. "That was thoughtful of you."

I beat back a wave of anxiety. Maybe if the detective saw that I was trying to be helpful, he'd clear me and let Benji and me finish our weekend. "Thank you. I thought so."

"About what time would you say you arrived at the canceled wedding?" the detective asked, and he looked far too interested in the answer.

"Around two-thirty, I would guess."

The detective nodded, like he had thought as much. "At ten minutes after two, we received an anonymous call that someone had been murdered in the hotel. Didn't give us a room number or a name. We kept it quiet as we had house-keeping check all the rooms. Didn't want to alarm the guests over nothing. They found no body. No blood. Figured it was a prank. Until you called us a few hours later."

"But...according to your time of death, that phone call had to have been made before he was killed."

Detective Holbrook raised both of his hands in a help-less gesture. "You see what I'm working with here? A man was reported dead before he actually died, and no one entered or left his room during the timeframe the murder must have occurred. Your conversation with the deceased in the hallway and your fingerprints are the only concrete things I have to go on."

"Oh, dear," I murmured. This wasn't looking good for

me. I threw an anxious glance at the detective. "But you're not arresting me, right? I never entered his room. You said so yourself. No one entered."

The detective frowned, like he was wondering why I was asking. "No, I'm not arresting you. Not yet."

I didn't like the fact that it was still a very real possibility, but at least I had some time to try to get myself out of this mess.

"How do you know your killer hasn't already left the resort?" I asked, realizing that if I had just murdered someone, I wouldn't stick around for the investigation.

Detective Holbrook's lips twitched up. It was the first hint of a smile I'd seen since meeting the detective. "Believe it or not, Ms. Swallows, I have investigated a murder before. All wedding guests are booked in their rooms until at least tomorrow, and, like you, we have asked them to stay at the resort until we've finished our preliminary round of questioning."

"And if you don't find your murderer before checkout tomorrow?"

The small smile that had appeared immediately disappeared, and the detective leaned forward. "For all I know, I'm looking at her."

Ouch.

"Well, you know where to find me if you have any additional questions," I said, moving to stand.

Detective Holbrook stood with me. "And you can be

assured that I will have questions. This investigation is far from over."

I was afraid of that.

IT TOOK ALL of twenty seconds after leaving the security office for my mother to call. Honestly, I was surprised it had taken that long. The Amor gossip train was usually more efficient than that.

"You should never have gone to that wedding," my mother started, in lieu of pleasantries. "From the way Coral says it, she heard from Janice that it was a disaster from start to finish."

I didn't know who either of those people were, but they'd gotten the gossip right. Unfortunately, the wedding weekend was far from over.

"Yes, Mom, it could have gone better."

"And then for Mark to be murdered. Can you imagine being a widow on your wedding day? Do what you can to comfort the poor woman, but don't stay any longer than you need to. That family has proven to be a curse since they first set foot in Amor."

Looked like Coral and Janice hadn't gotten all the gossip right. Like the fact that the wedding had been canceled before Mark had even died, and I was unsure how devastated Bree really was.

I hadn't told my mom the bad news about my having to stay an additional day, hoping everything would work itself out by morning and Benji and I would be free to go.

It hadn't worked out that way, though, and I could no longer delay the inevitable. "They're still investigating what happened, so we'll be staying an extra day. Will you guys be okay until tomorrow?"

Benji exited the office, and his gaze swept the hallway, landing on me. His lips were pressed in a tight line.

"Of course we'll be okay, but why do they need you another day?" my mom demanded.

I couldn't tell her anything about my involvement in the investigation. My mom jumping in the car and storming up to the resort was the last thing we needed right now. I'd be more likely to be arrested than not if she put herself in the middle of things.

"Just as a precaution. They've asked all the guests to stay."

"You're letting the police do their job, aren't you?" she asked. "You're not trying to be Sherlock or anything like that?"

Considering my propensity to get myself caught up in these kinds of situations, I could understand her concern. "The police have it under control, Mom." That was sort of true. They were working on it. As far as if they truly had it under control, well, I was their prime suspect. So, I couldn't say I was impressed with their skills.

My mom didn't seem convinced as she harrumphed. "All right, but I don't want you staying a moment longer than necessary. You don't need to be involved with all the negativity that family brings with them."

"I've met them. They aren't bad people."

"That's because you don't remember what it was like when you were young," my mom started.

Before she could go off on all the ways the Garrett family had wronged us, I hurriedly moved to end the conversation. "I love you, Mom. But I have to go. See you tomorrow. Give my love to the kids. Oh, and be nice to Trish."

I hung up just before we reached the elevator, my mom still grumbling about not understanding why I needed to stay another night, considering there was a murderer on the loose. Probably after all the wedding guests.

Before I had the chance to think on that last statement, Benji and I stepped off onto the ninth floor and walked toward our room, exhausted from the detective's never-ending questions.

I stopped mid-step.

Someone was waiting for us.

8

A man I recognized from the wedding stood outside our door, waiting. It looked as if he'd knocked but there had been no answer, and he was now trying to decide what to do.

It was the man who had been arguing with the young woman in the jade dress. He glanced our way, and his expression brightened. "Maddie Swallows. I've been looking all over for you," he said, meeting us halfway down the hallway. He stuck out a hand. "Robert Peters."

That was a very old name for such a young guy.

"Any relation to Mark Peters?" I asked. There was no way he wasn't. He had the same Disney prince look going on that Mark had had, if Mark hadn't been drunk and looking homeless. He'd had the potential.

Aladdin's bronze complexion and slight frame. Flynn Rider's chiseled jaw. Prince Eric's sweeping hair. I half expected Robert to burst into song, right there in the hallway.

I wondered what he was doing at our hotel room and could think of no other reason than the supposition that the entire hotel had already heard about Benji and my interrogation with the detective, and this Robert Peters was here to do the same. Accuse me of murder.

"Mark is my older brother," Robert said. He hesitated. "I know you must have been at the so-called wedding yesterday. It was a circus, was what it was. But it goes far beyond a bride duping the wedding guests into thinking she actually loved my brother. I believe she allowed their relationship to progress all the way to the altar for more sinister reasons. Yesterday, Bree disappeared in the chaos, and Mark was killed in his hotel room shortly after. She murdered Mark."

I blinked. "Come again?"

"Cops are swarming the hotel. Everyone is being interviewed," Robert said, his breaths quick. "If they haven't gotten to you yet, they will. They're determined to make an arrest before everyone leaves tomorrow. But my room is on the same hallway as Bree. I saw how the cops interacted with her—treated her like the grieving fiancée. They're looking in all the wrong places, and no one has their finger pointed at her. I know she did it, though."

It was possible, but I wasn't so sure. "What does this have to do with me, Mr. Peters?"

"My parents—they haven't left their hotel room since

they got the news. Heartbroken doesn't come close to how Mark's death has affected them. They need closure. And I need justice."

Robert couldn't possibly be suggesting what I thought he was. "I still don't understand."

His gaze jumped from me to Benji and back again. "I know this is unfair to ask of you—I understand that you grew up with Bree and her family. But Mr. Garrett mentioned in passing that you are the best psychologist in the state and that you've helped solve two murders. Or was it three? In any case, you can prove Bree did this."

I doubted that was what Mr. Garrett had intended when he'd mentioned my accomplishments to Robert, considering that Bree was his daughter.

This was a big ask. And something I had no desire to do. "And if Bree didn't do it?"

Robert hesitated, as if he hadn't considered that as an option. "Then you need to find who is responsible."

When I glanced at Benji, he gave a quick shake of his head.

And I agreed.

"Mr. Peters, you do realize that I'm not a detective, right? It sounds like the cops are taking care of it. Not to mention the small fact that the real detective is convinced I'm the one who murdered Mark, not Bree. I doubt I'll be useful in this particular situation."

It was Robert's turn to stare. "What?"

Okay, so he hadn't heard.

"Maddie was the last person to speak with Mark before he died, so the detective has taken a special interest in her," Benji answered for me, and I was grateful for it. I wouldn't have put it so nicely.

Robert's lips parted in surprise. "But that's preposterous."

"I was alone for close to an hour while Benji was up in our hotel room. And because I was down at the wedding venue, even though it was for only a few minutes, I had access to the murder weapon."

"The cake knife." His eyes narrowed. "What a terrible way to end a man's life, on his wedding day no less. What kind of person does something like that?"

My thoughts raced, uninvited, my psychology training kicking into gear.

It made sense that the killer was one of the wedding guests. Maybe a jealous ex-girlfriend. Considering the irony, it was probably someone who was trying to make a statement. Except, they'd returned the murder weapon and buried the body in the dunes. That would defeat the purpose of any symbolic statement they were trying to make.

I shook away the thoughts. No. I wasn't doing this again. I wasn't going after a murderer. I had to trust that the local law enforcement were good at their jobs and could find whoever had killed Mark. This wasn't my home-town, and any snooping could land me in a worse position than I was already in.

"You know, when I was talking with the cop who interviewed me," Robert mused, "I asked him why they didn't just check the security cameras. He said they did, but the wedding cake was blocking the view of the knife. Couldn't get a clear shot of who took it."

And my prints were on it.

I forced myself to take a long breath. It was fine. No problem. The detective didn't have anything concrete on me, otherwise I'd still be down in the security office. They'd find Mark's killer.

Except, no one else had entered or left Mark's room all day.

There was no one else.

I had to find who had really done it, or it was going to end up being me.

"ARE you sure you want to do this?" Benji asked as we rode the elevator back down to the lobby. It had taken all of five minutes in our lavish hotel suite to realize that there would be no way I could relax until Mark's murderer was in the custody of Detective Holbrook. And that meant having a little conversation with Mark's ex-fiancée. Only problem was that I had no idea where to find her.

"What else am I supposed to do?" I asked him, stepping out of the elevator. "I know you were friends with Bree, but that doesn't mean we can automatically assume she is innocent."

Benji frowned. "Robert's assumption doesn't mean she's guilty, either."

No, it didn't. But I couldn't tell Benji as much because we nearly bowled Mr. Garrett over as he was walking in from outside.

"Benji," Mr. Garrett exclaimed, a grin erupting over his face. "I was beginning to wonder when I'd see you." He pulled Benji into a familial hug. Benji returned it but threw me a strained smile as he did.

His expression was clear. He didn't want me investigating anywhere near the Garrett family.

Unlike Robert, Mark's death hadn't seemed to affect Mr. Garrett in the slightest. And that was concerning to me.

"I was just finishing getting the wedding venue squared away. What a mess," Mr. Garrett said, steering us toward the overstuffed chairs in the lounge area. "But come, we must catch up. How are your parents doing?" he asked Benji.

"They're doing fine. Still living in Amor, of course. Will be until the day they die."

Mr. Garrett laughed. "I believe it. They always had a soft spot for our little town." He paused, his smile dipping. "I suppose the police have been by to speak with you?"

I was unsure how much Mr. Garrett knew, or how much he needed to know, so I simply gave a small nod.

He released a long sigh. "You know you should be the

one running the investigation, Maddie. I've heard you have quite the success rate."

"Word gets around," I said.

Mr. Garrett's eyes crinkled in amusement. "I still have my connections in Amor."

I raised a shoulder. "It seems the police already have everything under control. Is everyone who attended the wedding still here?"

"Everyone except Melinda and Daniel," Mr. Garrett said. "They took off mid-wedding. They had some things they needed to attend to."

That was a strange way to put it, considering there hadn't been a wedding. Not only that, but Melinda was probably the maid of honor. Why would they leave in the middle of her sister's wedding?

"She okay?" I asked, trying to sound casual.

Mr. Garrett stayed quiet, as if he had to think about it. "I hope so," he finally answered. "She and Daniel have some things to work out, and I'll admit that yesterday wasn't the best timing for it. Or maybe it was perfect timing, all things considered."

Meaning they hadn't been here for Bree's canceled wedding and her fiancé's murder. And they couldn't be considered suspects.

Benji gave me a warning look. He knew what I was doing—trying to get information. But I had to, didn't I? Not for closure, like Mr. and Mrs. Peters. Or a sense of justice, like Robert. But for self-preservation. I had no intention of going to jail for something I hadn't done.

"What do you say, Maddie? Can I hire you to find who killed Mark? Money isn't an issue."

That was awfully generous, considering that Mr. Garrett hadn't been overly fond of Mark when we'd spoken just one day earlier.

"You don't trust Detective Holbrook?" I asked.

Mr. Garrett didn't answer right away. "Mark's father is my business partner. A good man. He and his wife don't deserve this. And the sooner it gets taken care of, the better."

Business partner?

My gaze found Benji, and I wondered if he had known how Mark had been connected to the Garretts. He looked as surprised as I felt.

"I'm not a professional detective, Mr. Garrett. I could never accept money." I paused. "You said that Mr. Peters is your business partner. Is that how Mark and Bree met? Through you?"

Mr. Garrett gave a curt nod. "Yes, unfortunately."

"How would a canceled wedding between your children affect your business relationship with Mr. Peters?" I asked, unable to help myself. That didn't seem like the kind of thing that would end well.

"It wouldn't have affected a thing," Mr. Garrett assured me. "In fact, it would have actually made things easier if they'd broken up months ago. Yes, we sort of set the kids up on a date, but it was more that we were all going out to dinner to celebrate. Nick Peters and I decided to break away from our firm and launch our own company. It was my wife and me, Nick and his wife, and our two children. I hadn't meant for anything like this wedding to happen. Mark and Bree were all wrong for each other from the start."

"And does Mr. Peters feel the same way?"

Mr. Garrett surprised me by chuckling. "Oh, yes. Nick hadn't broken the news to his son that he wouldn't be joining us at the new firm—something Mark had been counting on. With him and Bree getting married, it complicated things."

A complication. But certainly not motive for murder.

"So tragic for it to be resolved in this way," Benji said.

"A tragedy for sure," Mr. Garrett agreed. "Whatever my feelings toward the boy, it wasn't right that his life was taken from him like that." He stood from his chair, indicating that our time together was finished.

When I attempted to get out of my overstuffed chair, however, I found myself having to practically crawl out of it. Benji threw me a smirk, stood up like it was the easiest thing in the world, and held out a hand to me.

I accepted his offer, relishing the feel of the calluses on his hand as he pulled me up. My ex-husband had never had calluses. Such was the life of an academic in his ivory tower.

Mr. Garrett took a step forward and rested a hand on

my arm. "I do hope you'll consider looking into the investigation. It would mean a lot to me."

"I understand," I said, unsure if I should say anything about Robert Peters requesting the same thing of me just minutes earlier. But then I'd likely let it slip that Robert suspected Bree of the crime. When Mr. Garrett's lips turned down in disappointment at my reluctance, I added, "If there is a way to help, I will."

Benji didn't let go of my hand as the three of us walked toward the elevators. I liked to think it was to let me know he was there, whatever happened. At least, I hoped that was what it meant.

Mr. Garrett stopped and pushed the UP button. "I trust you'll keep this between us?"

"Of course," I said.

Mr. Garrett's gaze landed somewhere beyond me, and his face seemed to pale by a few shades. "Look, if you need to get ahold of me, text me at this number." He reached into his jacket pocket and produced a business card. I wondered if men like him always kept their cards handy, just in case. I took it, but when the elevator doors opened, rather than join us, he hurried away toward the hotel lobby. "Any time of day," he said over his shoulder, as if it were an afterthought.

I watched Mr. Garrett disappear around a corner, then turned back to Benji. "That was..."

"Strange?" he finished for me.

Yeah, that was a good way to put it.

"I need to take on this investigation, Benji."

He didn't respond right away. Not until we were inside the elevator and the doors had closed.

"I guess the question comes down to, do you trust the detective to look beyond the obvious?" Benji said.

Beyond the obvious. Meaning me.

"I don't have the luxury of trusting him. Not with all the evidence he has."

Benji gave me a resigned look, like he'd expected that response. "We should probably start with Bree, then."

I tried to hide my surprise, but I didn't think I was successful, considering how amused he looked.

He lifted a shoulder. "I figure if you talk to her first, you'll see how wrong Robert is about her, and then we can move on to the real suspects."

"All right," I said, then silently added, *assuming you aren't wrong and she didn't murder her fiancé.*

9

I really didn't want to call Mr. Garrett to ask where we might find Bree. If he thought we were investigating his daughter, he might not be so willing to help us. But the only information we had was that, according to Robert Peters, her room was on the fifth floor. There were a lot of rooms on each floor, and going around and knocking on each of them could only get us into trouble with the detective—not something I needed at the moment.

As I attempted to put off the phone call, Benji and I sat on the balcony, our gazes settled on the pristine white sand in the distance, and I wished this moment could last forever.

But like most good things, it came to an end all too soon.

"Call him," Benji said. He placed a hand on my knee, and my gaze found his. It was in these moments that even the slightest of touches did me in. Benji and I had always been comfortable with each other, and I'd never thought anything of it growing up. But over the past couple of years...it meant something.

And I knew it meant something to Benji as well. At least, it had in the past.

And last night.

But did it now?

I shook myself from the thoughts. That was not the priority right now. "Okay. I'll call him."

Pulling out Mr. Garrett's business card, I entered the number on my phone.

Ringing.

"Hello?"

A pause. I could do this.

"Mr. Garrett, it's Maddie. We are hoping to get more context around yesterday's events. I know that Bree must be having a terrible time right now, but do you think it would be possible for us to speak with her?"

Mr. Garrett began talking, but it seemed to be directed toward someone else in the room with him, his words muffled.

"She'd be happy to. Her room is right next to Mark's. Room 529. Can you meet her there in fifteen minutes?"

Interesting that Bree and Mark hadn't shared a room, or at least hadn't had a suite like Benji and I, considering they would have been husband and wife by now.

"We'll be there, Mr. Garrett. Thank you."

. . .

EVEN THOUGH THE fifth floor looked exactly the same as every other floor in the hotel, when Benji and I stepped off the elevator, memories of my encounter with Mark washed over me. How unhappy he'd seemed. Looking for anything that could distract him from his reality. And how I'd felt like I couldn't get away fast enough, no matter how sorry I felt for the man.

"You okay?" Benji asked, his brow creased in concern.

I forced a smile. "Yeah, great. Just hoping that Bree can tell us something that will be helpful."

Benji gave me a skeptical look. He knew I was holding back, but he didn't push it. Instead, he led me to room 529 and gave two sharp raps on the door.

It immediately swung open, and a woman with dark hair stood on the other side. She looked familiar, but I wouldn't have done a double take passing her on the street. Wouldn't have recognized her from my childhood. She definitely had Melinda's complexion, though, and her dad's eyes.

"Thank you so much for coming," Bree said, opening the door wider and motioning for us to come in.

"I'm sorry it's under these circumstances," I said, walking past her. The hotel room was smaller than Benji's and mine but had the same distinct feeling of elegance.

"As am I." Bree closed the door behind us, then walked toward a sofa and love seat in a far corner of the room near the window. "It makes me anxious staying another night when I know a murderer was on this floor. And hasn't been caught. But you're here, so that's something, isn't it." She turned to Benji. "How have you been, Benny? It's been a while."

It could have been my imagination, but I swore a blush crept up Benji's neck. And since when did anyone call him Benny?

"Yes, but that's through no fault of my own," he said. "It seems everyone can't escape Amor fast enough."

I bristled and tried to not take the comment personally. It was true that a lot of people left; I wasn't the only one. But it seemed to still be a sore point for Benji. And maybe the thing that had been keeping our relationship from moving forward.

He brought it up so often, maybe he was afraid I would leave again.

Bree raised a shoulder, conceding his point. "It's true. But the grass isn't necessarily greener where I ended up. In fact, right now, it's looking quite brown."

"That's why we're here," I said. "Your dad seems to think I can find Mark's murderer. I tried to warn him, because truthfully, I don't know how much good I'll be able to do. I didn't know Mark, or anyone else at the wedding. I also don't have access to security cameras, and I can't go around interviewing people like the police can."

"And yet, the cops seem to be pointing all their attention in the wrong direction," Bree interjected. "When the detective sat me down for questioning, he asked about you specifically. Asked what your connection to Mark was." She shook her head. "I told him there wasn't a connection, but he wouldn't listen. Seems like they're trying to wrap up this investigation fast. Guess it doesn't look great for a fancy resort to have law enforcement poking around too long, huh?"

"No, I suppose it doesn't." Now, how to ask questions without seeming like I was accusing her of anything. "Bree, did you hear any noise from next door? Even something that didn't seem important at the time?"

She was shaking her head before I'd even finished the question. "I was downstairs for the wedding. Didn't hear a thing."

Benji and I shared a look of confusion.

"I don't understand," I said, my words slow. "Even though Mark was under the impression that the wedding had simply been delayed, in reality, there wasn't going to be a wedding. If you knew this, why go downstairs at the original time? Why was Mark the only one missing?"

Bree opened her mouth to respond but must have come up empty, because she clamped her lips shut, and her gaze traveled to the window overlooking the sand dunes.

"It all fell apart so fast," she finally said, her voice quiet.

Benji leaned forward, his elbows on his knees. "The wedding?"

"I never wanted to marry him." Bree's gaze returned to

us. "Don't know how it got to this point, really. What started as a blind date spiraled into more dates, and before I knew it, I was engaged." She paused. "My parents seemed so happy about the arrangement. Couldn't ask for a better match, right?"

Bree released a laugh that was devoid of any humor, then fell silent.

"Did Mark know how you felt?" I asked, knowing I was treading on dangerous ground. This was where my patients either opened up or shut down. But Bree seemed like she was practically bursting with pent-up anger. The type that she hadn't been able to share and was grateful to finally release. And because Benji and I had no skin in the game, we were the perfect ones to share the burden.

To my surprise, Bree's eyes darkened, all that anger contorting her features into hate. Loathing. The type I'd seen in Mark the previous day.

"Oh, he knew, all right," Bree said. "I tried breaking off the engagement, but he refused to accept it. Our fathers are leaving their tech firm and starting their own consulting company. Mark wanted a place at the new business, and he said that if we broke off the engagement, both our fathers' business and his aspirations would be jeopardized. Never mind that Mark didn't care for me at all, didn't even deny cheating on me for who knows how long with his dad's secretary. Said we could have an 'open relationship' after we were married."

The resentment was palpable in her voice. And was pure motive for murder.

"You could have just taken off the ring and said, 'Too bad,'" Benji said.

That had been the wrong thing to say.

Bree turned on Benji, her eyes flashing. "You didn't know Mark. He was ambitious. And rich. And used to getting what he wanted, when he wanted it. In short, I was scared of him. But by the end, I didn't care anymore. The thought of walking down the aisle with him made me want to throw up." She pulled in a shuddered breath, like she was attempting to regain control. "As it turned out, my dad didn't like Mark any more than I did. He told Mark that the wedding had been postponed to buy us some time. Dad was going to break the news to Mark's family and smooth things over, and I would slip away before Mark realized what was happening."

An abusive relationship. Also motive for murder. For some women, they believed it was the only way out of the marriage. "What did Mark's parents think of the match?"

Bree stood, wrapping her arms around her stomach, and walked over to the large window.

"They were thrilled, and why wouldn't they be?" She tossed back a wry smile. "I'm a great catch."

I nodded and stared at the blank notebook in my hand. "So, if I understand it correctly, Mark was the only one who thought the wedding was postponed. You were outside with the rest of the guests, doing what? Waiting for the wedding that you knew wasn't going to happen?"

"Not exactly." She hesitated. "Even if I'm not meant for a happily-ever-after, any fool with eyes could see that Melinda and her friend, Daniel, were perfect for each other. Our family and friends were already here. It made sense for them to take my and Mark's places."

My lips parted in surprise, and I didn't know what to say to that. I was having trouble picturing Melinda settling down with anyone, let alone Daniel, the man who had helped clean up broken dishes a few weeks ago. I'd known they were friends, and she'd certainly seemed different when she was with him.

But still. An impromptu marriage?

When I couldn't find the words, Benji stepped in.

"So, that's why Melinda and Daniel left early? Running away to their honeymoon?"

Bree shook her head and gave us a sad smile. "My mother and grandmother had not been privy to the plans and intervened. Unfortunately, two weddings were canceled yesterday. Daniel left first, and Melinda went chasing after him."

Oy, talk about drama. Could this weekend handle any more?

"There must have been a lot of distractions," I said, still left with a blank notebook. What was important here? What could prove that I hadn't killed Mark? "Anyone could have slipped away unnoticed."

"Oh, yes, plenty of distraction. Funny thing was, our dad's business associates seemed to be angrier than our families were. Maybe they considered it a waste of their time. Thought they would be here furthering their careers, and instead they got two failed weddings and a murder. Not exactly good for business, especially because some of my dad's biggest clients were here."

Okay, maybe that was something I could work with.

"Any of them angry enough to kill?"

Bree saw where I was taking this line of questioning, and she slumped back onto the sofa. "I'm sorry, Maddie. I thought I could be of help, but I realize now that I probably know less than you do. I didn't recognize most of the people at the wedding. I didn't see anyone take the cake knife. And I don't know anyone who hated Mark more than myself."

And then there was that.

10

"I'm sorry, but I don't believe she did it," Benji said as we walked away from Bree's room.

I didn't like to think she was capable of something so awful either, but we had to face the facts. "I know," I said. "But she was in an abusive relationship with a man she didn't love. He was blatantly cheating on her and tried to threaten her with his money and ruining her dad's career. Who knows, he might have even been physically abusive. I mean, Bree said she was scared of the guy. And after my one chance meeting with him, I can totally see it. He scared me too. Bree felt trapped. Desperate. That can make people do things they'd never considered before."

Benji had been nodding this whole time, showing me he was listening, but I could tell he wasn't changing his mind. "If Mark can invoke such fear and hatred, it's likely that there is a whole host of people who had motive, right?"

"True," I said, my words slow. The thought that it was very possible Bree hadn't done it should have been comforting. Instead, it was overwhelming. We didn't have the time or the means to speak with an entire guest list to see who hated Mark the most.

We stopped in front of the elevators but hadn't had time to push the DOWN button when it dinged and the doors opened.

Revealing Detective Holbrook.

He took a step back in surprise but quickly regained his composure and walked past us into the hallway. "Interesting finding you two here on the fifth floor, considering your room is on the ninth," he said. "Checking if you missed anything incriminating at the crime scene?"

"I suppose that's what one would do if they were guilty," I said, forcing myself to hold the detective's gaze. "But no, we were checking in on a friend. Making sure she was doing okay, you know, considering her fiancé was murdered yesterday."

Detective Holbrook nodded in understanding. "Oh, yes. Bree Garrett. I'm on my way to speak with her now."

"Oh?" I tried not to sound too interested. "New information that you need to share with her? Personally, I bet it was the maid who did it."

Benji shot me an amused look, and I could admit that I had resorted to the immature tactic of goading. But I couldn't help myself. The detective had been incredibly frustrating up to this point, not interested whatsoever in helping prove my innocence.

And as it turned out, the tactic ended up being quite effective.

The detective stopped so fast, he nearly tumbled, and his gaze whipped toward me. "Who told you about the maid?"

"Uh. I—" I'd never been good at thinking on my feet, and my brain seized up, refusing to come up with any decent response. The detective took my loss for words as a sign of not wanting to tell him what I knew. Which was nothing. But he didn't need to know that.

"I told them not to share that security footage with anyone," the detective murmured, his brows dipped in frustration. "But I should have known better. No one cares about the sanctity of an investigation anymore."

"I'm ready for my apology now. I told you I didn't do it." And now I was just getting annoyingly presumptuous. Even Benji was giving me a warning look not to push this further. I supposed I now knew where my kids had gotten it from.

The detective's gaze returned to me. "Just because we have the maid entering the room earlier in the day, and not leaving, it doesn't mean anything. She had to have left at some point, considering we didn't find a maid hiding under the bed when we searched the room. I'm sorry, Ms. Swallows, but you are not yet off the hook."

I had ruffled the detective's feathers. Good. He didn't give me the chance to ruffle any more as he spun away and stalked down the hall toward Bree's room. Poor woman was being accosted from every side.

There wasn't much I could do to help Bree with that one. But I did need to figure out which of the maids had been in Mark's bedroom yesterday morning.

I felt the sudden need for an extra blanket from housekeeping. From what I had heard, it was going to be a cold night.

I SET the hotel phone down in its cradle and smiled. "One extra blanket coming right up."

Benji was pacing, not looking nearly as pleased with my efforts as I was. "I don't like this."

"What is it exactly that you don't like? The fact that a murderer is roaming free in this hotel, or the fact that the police still think I did it?"

Benji walked up to me with an intensity I didn't think I'd ever seen in him. He grabbed both of my hands in his and looked me in the eyes. "I don't like that you keep getting yourself in these situations. I don't like that you could be in danger and that the more people you talk to, the more likely the killer will hear of it. You could be making them antsy. Antsy people do dangerous things." He sucked in a breath. "And I don't like that this is what our relationship has become. Me being worried about you."

Benji was gripping my hands so tightly now—with such urgency—that I had to pry my fingers from his.

"I don't mean to," I said, my voice soft. "This weekend didn't turn out how we'd expected, and certainly not how I wanted."

He released a defeated sigh and retreated to the couch. "I know. I just—" Benji ran a hand through his hair. "I feel guilty for encouraging you in these investigations. If anything were to happen to you…"

I sank onto the couch next to him. "I wish I could just pretend everything is wonderful. That we're having a fabulous weekend getaway at a beautiful resort. Just you and me. No murders. No dead bodies. I do."

Benji nodded. "But you can't pretend. And you shouldn't. I wouldn't want you to." He paused. "Just do me a favor and be careful. Don't go questioning people on your own."

When I gave him a look that said, *Would I do that?* his lips quirked up.

"It's what you do, Maddie. And you don't have Sheriff Potts here as backup this time."

It was true; I tended to act first, think later. "Guess that means you are my designated partner in crime," I said, nudging him with my shoulder.

He laughed as he shook his head. I could tell that he

wasn't exactly excited about being mixed up in another murder investigation. "Guess I am."

A knock on the door. "Housekeeping. I have your extra blanket," came the muffled voice.

Benji and I both stood from the couch.

"'Kay, partner. You taking the lead on this one?" Benji asked.

I gave a quick nod.

Except, it wasn't a maid waiting for me when I opened the door.

11

"Elijah," I said, surprised to see the bellhop from earlier. He was holding a blanket and shuffling his feet, looking nervous. "I didn't realize your job description extended to blanket delivery."

Elijah's expression was one of unease as he held the blanket out to me. "It normally doesn't, ma'am, but housekeeping has been needing extra help the last couple of days."

"Because of the murder?" I guessed.

Elijah's lips parted in surprise, and even I was a little taken aback by my own bluntness. But we didn't have time to beat around the bush here.

"Yes, ma'am. The entire staff is spooked, and housekeeping visits every room in the resort, every single day. Which means that if the culprit is still here—"

"Then at least one of you will have contact with him," I finished for him. "I can see why you're nervous."

Elijah gave a rapid nod. "The maids have started visiting rooms in pairs, so they've needed more help than usual. I guess they figured I'd be okay on my own."

I held the door open and motioned inside. "I just need to find my purse. There's a couple of dollars in there that I can give you for your trouble."

Elijah glanced up and down the hallway. "I'll stay outside, ma'am. Not allowed to go inside the rooms. And I can't be long. They'll worry."

"Management?"

That finally earned me Elijah's infectious laugh. "No, ma'am. Don't think they care about catching the killer so much as want to get the police out of here. Say it's spooking the guests."

I gave him an understanding smile. "Why don't you give me the blanket?" I said when I noticed Elijah still clutching it as if it were a shield of protection.

He handed it to me, his gaze still jumpy.

"I'm sure management doesn't know half of what goes on in their hotel," I said offhandedly as I stepped back with the blanket.

I then purposely took more time than I needed retrieving my purse, because I was sure Elijah knew more than he realized. The resort's staff—they saw everything. Watched everything. Probably heard everything too.

Elijah gave another high-pitched laugh. "How right you are, ma'am."

I returned to the doorway as I rummaged in my purse for my wallet. "But you and the rest of the staff—you know everything and everyone inside and out."

Elijah was warming up, and he nodded vigorously. "We practically run the place." As soon as he said it, his eyes widened with horror and he threw a glance at Benji, who was behind me, leaning against the wall, listening with a slight smile. "I didn't mean that, ma'am. Not really."

I laughed as I pulled out the money. "It's okay, Elijah. Everyone knows who's really running the show. In fact, I bet you have some guesses on who the killer is. Don't believe the rumors that I did it, either. Completely false." I paused, realization settling over me. "Is that why you were so nervous to come up to our floor?"

Elijah hesitated, more cautious than he had been a moment earlier. "Honestly, ma'am, if I were to guess, I would have pegged the victim as the killer. Liked to throw his weight around, demand things from people without even a thank you. Tips are nice, sure, but respect is even better. And that guy didn't give out either one."

I *tssked* and shook my head. "I don't understand how people can be like that." I paused. "The detective told me he was looking into an incident with one of the maids. Is she all right?"

That wasn't a complete fabrication. The detective had

let it slip while talking to me. That had to count for something.

Elijah snorted. "That detective has been pestering staff all day but doesn't even know what he's looking for. It's like he hopes if he asks enough questions, someone will accidentally admit that they did it."

That gave me pause. "You mean, he thinks one of the staff members did it?"

Elijah raised a shoulder. "I guess. He was convinced that one of the maids was hiding something, because on the cameras, he saw that she had entered the victim's room but hadn't left. What the detective failed to realize was that the victim had reserved a room with a connecting door to his fiancée's room. They could open it up and expand the space anytime they wanted. Maybe they were old-fashioned and wanted separate rooms up until the wedding."

Somehow, I doubted that was the reason, considering everything Bree had told us. Sounded like Mark just hadn't wanted people getting suspicious when asking for separate bedrooms.

"So, when the maid entered the victim's room to clean, she proceeded into his fiancée's room and left from there?"

I'd forgotten I still held the money for Elijah's tip and handed it to him.

"Sure. The connecting door must have been left open," he said, slipping the bills into his pocket. "Otherwise, they treat it as two separate rooms, and she wouldn't have exited that way."

Bree had had access to Mark through her room. This wasn't looking good for her.

"Oh, man, I gotta get going," Elijah said when a female voice suddenly filled the hall, asking where Elijah was. I hadn't noticed the radio clipped to his side. "Thanks for the chat, ma'am. Always nice to feel appreciated." And then he was gone.

"What do you think?" Benji asked as I shut the door.

I was unsure and had to think on it for a moment.

"I think," I said, the words coming out slowly, "that no one liked Mark. But dealing with a rude guest isn't a reason for a staff member to kill him. Otherwise, half the people who come to the resort wouldn't make it out alive."

Benji nodded. "I agree."

So, who did that leave us with?

Bree.

Silence settled over us.

I STARED at the computer screen in front of me, my eyes starting to glaze over. "I'm sorry," I said to Benji when he walked up from behind me and peered over my shoulder. "Just a little longer, I promise."

I sat at the table in our hotel room, an emailed document open in front of me. After scrolling and scrolling and scrolling some more, I realized I had no idea what I'd gotten myself into when I'd asked Mr. Garrett for the wedding guest list. It had been a favor to Benji when I'd

requested the list, a promise that I'd look beyond the obvious. Look at all possibilities even when everything pointed
to Bree.

I wasn't going to take anything at face value.

Unlike the detective.

Two hundred names were on this list.

I laid my forehead on the table and sucked in a long
breath. What I needed was a break.

Getting up, I walked out to the balcony. The sun was
high in the sky, and its light reflected off the white sand in
the distance. I tilted my face up and closed my eyes,
allowing the warmth of the sun to wash over me.

I had been accused of murdering a man I didn't know,
and I wasn't any closer to figuring out who had done it.

But I was in a beautiful resort with my best friend. That
had to count for something.

As if my thoughts had summoned him, Benji followed
me out and rested his arms on the banister. He nudged me
with his shoulder.

"How you holding up?"

I'd thought I was doing okay. Until he'd asked.

I lowered my gaze and pulled in a shuddered breath. "I
don't even know anymore."

"We'll find whoever did it, I promise," Benji said. When
I didn't respond, he added, "Why don't we get you some
lunch? A full stomach always helps me think better."

I hadn't even realized how hungry I was until he'd

mentioned it. Now, my stomach protested at how long it had gone without sustenance.

"You're right. Food fixes everything," I said, allowing him to lead me back inside. "What do you think they did with all the food meant for the wedding dinner last night?"

Benji laughed. "That's more like the Maddie I know."

THE PREVIOUS EVENING, Benji and I had discovered exactly one restaurant where we could pronounce the names on the menu. Well, most of them, anyway. It wasn't casual dining, by any means, but it was the closest thing we'd get to it.

As we waited for the waiter to bring us our drinks, I watched Benji unfold the cloth napkin that held his utensils, then place it on his lap. Sometime in the past twenty years, he'd learned proper etiquette, something I'd never managed, and I followed suit as I placed my napkin on my own lap. I wondered if it had been Candace, his fiancée, who had taught him.

It didn't matter, really, and I didn't know why the thought had even presented itself. It was ridiculous to be jealous of a dead woman, but with all these new feelings toward Benji bombarding me, it was hard not to be.

When Benji glanced my way, a small smile tugging at his lips, I averted my gaze, as if by making eye contact, he'd know what had been running through my mind.

That was when I noticed a woman sitting at the next table. She was alone, and her eyes were red and puffy.

I tapped Benji's hand, then nodded toward the woman.

"Think she's from the wedding?" I asked, my voice low.

"Pretty good chance, I'd say."

My thoughts of Benji and his former fiancée fled as quickly as they had appeared as I considered approaching the woman to make sure she was okay.

She glanced up and noticed me watching her.

"What?" she asked with an annoyed tone. I saw now that she had mascara streaks on her cheeks, like she'd been crying for quite some time, and strands of red hair were pulled out of her ponytail at odd angles.

"I'm sorry," I said. "I just wanted to make sure you were all right." Before I could think better of it, I slid from my seat and into the chair directly across from her.

She looked surprised at my direct approach and wiped at her eyes with the back of her hand. I couldn't help but notice the diamond ring on her finger. It was so large, it looked like wearing it must have been quite the workout.

"I'm Maddie," I said, sticking my hand out.

She hesitated, throwing a glance over at Benji, like she was wondering if I could be trusted. He smiled and shrugged, as if he was used to me going up to random strangers in restaurants and making myself at home.

"Amanda," she finally said, shaking my hand. She may have thought it was the only way to get me to go away.

She was wrong, of course. It only encouraged me.

"Are you all right, Amanda?" I asked. "It looks like you've had a rough day."

Amanda looked like she was on the verge of more tears when she said, "If my fiancé dying is considered a rough day, then yes, it has been."

Okay, not a wedding ring. An engagement ring.

"How awful," I said. "I'm surprised you even managed to come down to eat at all. If it were me, I'd have holed up in my room with room service on speed dial." I was in full therapist mode now.

Amanda's shoulders relaxed, and she released a long breath. "Trust me, I was tempted."

"When were you supposed to be married?" I asked.

A waiter walked up with my and Benji's drinks, keeping Amanda from answering, and he seemed confused on where to deliver them. I glanced in Amanda's direction. "Why don't you join our table? You really shouldn't be alone."

Her lips tilted up. A small victory.

"Thank you."

The waiter moved Amanda's place settings over, and she settled in next to me. "We didn't have an exact date," she said, continuing our conversation after taking a sip of her water. It seemed to help calm her nerves. "We were thinking next summer, though. There were some family complications—they didn't exactly approve of our relationship."

"That surprises me," I said. "You seem like a great

catch."

"Oh, I am," she said quickly. "It was...complicated. We were hoping to get everything ironed out over the next few months." Her gaze dropped to the table. "Guess they win this round. No wedding after all."

I couldn't imagine Amanda's family being relieved that someone was dead, even if it meant the dissolution of the engagement. An uncomfortable silence settled over us, and for once, I didn't know what to say. It wasn't until our food arrived that Amanda's mood lifted, and she was soon chattering on about how beautiful the resort was.

I had been right. Food fixes everything.

Amanda's mood had improved so much that by the end of our meal, she seemed to have completely forgotten the tragedy she'd recently experienced. Until we stood to leave.

That was when the tears returned. They were so intense that she seemed unable to even stand. "I'm sorry," she said between sobs. "I just hate the thought of returning to our empty hotel room. Knowing this was supposed to be a romantic getaway."

I immediately felt guilty, leaving her alone like this. When I shared a glance with Benji, he gave a subtle shake of his head. He knew what my eyes had been asking. If we should invite her to hang out with us for the afternoon. But as much as I wanted to help her, I knew that now wasn't the time for company.

Like it or not, Benji and I had a murder to solve. Otherwise, we would have much bigger problems than the guilt of not sticking around and comforting a grieving woman.

"I believe they have an outdoor movie tonight," I gently suggested, and Benji's shoulders visibly relaxed. He'd been sure I'd invite her along on our manhunt. "Free drinks and a comedy might be just what you need."

Amanda's tears slowed. "You're right. A distraction would do me some good." She gave me a grateful smile and stood. "Thank you for your kindness."

As I watched her walk away, I couldn't help but feel like I should have done more.

Benji walked over and rested his hand on my lower back. "You did what you could. But now it's time you take care of yourself. For your own family."

He was right, of course.

I looked up to where he towered over me. Even after all these years, I always forgot how much taller than me he was. Seven inches didn't sound like a lot, until Benji was standing right next to me.

"All right," I said, squaring my shoulders. "Where to next?" I glanced at my phone. Three o'clock already. If the hotel was only holding the wedding guests until tomorrow, we had a lot of work ahead of us.

But it had to be done.

Because, of everyone who was hurting today, everyone who had cared about Mark and couldn't understand how such a senseless tragedy could occur—I was the one who needed to find his killer the most.

12

Benji and I had just left the restaurant when my phone rang. Flash's name appeared on the screen, and dread washed over me. My son wasn't the type to make social calls.

"Hey, buddy. What's up?"

Without preamble, Flash asked, "You near your laptop?"

"No, but I could be."

Flash didn't respond right away, instead talking to someone in the background. Something about chocolate chips. "I emailed you something that I thought might be useful, considering your current situation," he said when he returned. "Of course, I don't have all of the details, so I didn't know exactly what I was looking for, but it's a start."

My stomach fell, and I was afraid of what I might find in my inbox. "My current situation?"

"Well, yeah. You're involved in another murder, right? I heard Grandma talking to Trish."

I was torn between fear of what had been discussed and relief that my mom and Trish were actually on speaking terms.

"What did you do, Flash? Nothing illegal, I hope."

Flash yelled to someone that they could take his turn and that he'd be back in a minute, and then came the pounding of feet on stairs. The background noise quieted, but rather than answer my question, Flash asked, "You at your computer yet?"

Benji and I were just stepping into the elevator. "No. Should be at it in a couple of minutes. Mind giving me a heads up of what I should expect?"

Flash was quiet for a moment. "Let me preface things by saying, if the hotel didn't want me accessing their cameras, they should have stronger security around them. Honestly, they're more of a scare tactic than anything."

I sucked in a long breath, trying to keep my frustration in check. Flash was just trying to help. I doubted the police would see it that way, though. "I don't think they're just a scare tactic, honey. The police have been scouring the camera feeds. Is there any way they will know if someone outside the hotel has been accessing the footage?"

"I doubt it. The security team there probably only knows how to access the video, not any of the background IT stuff. By the way, that is a really nice place you're staying at. How's the food?" A pause. "Never mind, don't tell me. I don't want to know what I'm missing out on." Another beat. "But it's amazing, right?"

I couldn't help but laugh as Benji and I entered our suite. "Okay, I'm here."

It didn't take long to power up my computer and pull up my email. And there, sitting at the top, were multiple emails from Flash.

"Why did you send so many things?"

"Because my email didn't allow me to send everything at once. It's amazing the amount of space these videos take up."

I opened the first one, and my breath caught. It was security feed from the fifth floor on the day of the murder. There was Mark, sitting in the hallway, drinking. The man that had entered the elevator as I'd been stepping out was there. An argument of some kind.

I fast-forwarded it, and I saw myself approach Mark. Fast-forwarded again until Mark re-entered his room.

"How did you know to check the fifth floor, and at what time?" I asked Flash, impressed by his skills.

A long sigh from the other end of the line. "Honestly, Mom, it's like you don't even know me."

It was true that Flash had incredible computer skills and I should have stopped being surprised years earlier by the things he could do.

"I'm sorry, honey. I should know better."

"Yes, you should," Flash said. "But really, I just checked

the hotel's log and searched for your victim's name. And there he was, on the fifth floor."

More fast-forwarding. Housekeeping was arriving now, ready to check rooms for a body that they'd never find.

"You good to go?" Flash asked. I was so invested in the video feed, I'd nearly forgotten I was still on the phone with him. "Trish is teaching us how to make homemade ice cream. We don't have an actual ice cream machine, so we've had to get creative. Hope you don't mind."

I was unsure what that meant, and it was probably better that I didn't know.

"Oh, yeah, sure. Sounds like fun." I hesitated before saying, "And thanks for the help. I appreciate knowing that you have my back, even when you can't be here." I probably shouldn't have been thanking him for hacking into the resort's security feed, but frankly, he'd done worse, and I could use any help I could get.

"Mom, one last thing," Flash said. "This Mark guy, I heard that he was killed with a cake knife, which is brutal all on its own. But does that mean no one actually got to eat the cake because it's now in evidence?"

"Sorry, buddy, no cake for us."

He blew out a long breath. "Such a waste."

ANXIETY WELLED as I searched the security videos for any kind of clue that could help us. As much as I appreciated Flash's unsolicited assistance, I now understood why the security feed hadn't been all that useful for Detective Holbrook.

With no audio, I was struggling to find anything that could help us discover who the killer was...or at least prove that I hadn't done it.

With a frustrated growl, I slammed my computer shut.

This was not the weekend I'd wanted.

And it was all Mark Peters' fault.

He had ruined it when he'd gotten himself killed.

It wasn't exactly fair for me to blame him for my predicament. He was dead, after all.

But there was still that part of me that said if he hadn't been such a horrible person whom everyone hated, no one would have felt the need to kill him.

I'd been so engrossed in my search of the videos Flash had sent me that Benji had left the suite at some point without me even realizing. My anger at Mark intensified.

And then my phone burst into song.

I snatched it from the table beside me. Disappointment replaced my anger when I saw it wasn't Benji.

Instead, an unfamiliar phone number was displayed on the screen. I was unsure if I should answer it, but I knew that it would drive me bonkers if I didn't take the call, always wondering who it had been. And I'd never have the guts to actually call the person back.

I took the plunge.

"Hello?"

A pause. But I could hear breathing.

"Maddie, it's Bree. When you came by earlier, I didn't tell you everything." Her words were quick and her breathing heavy. "After speaking with the detective earlier, I feel that I have no choice. I'd hoped this problem would go away on its own, but it's clear that it isn't."

This problem. Like it was a nuisance we were dealing with and not murder.

"Would you like to meet up somewhere?" I asked. "Maybe the pool?" I'd really prefer a public place. Because even though Benji was convinced Bree hadn't done it, I was coming up short on suspects.

"No," Bree said quickly, her tone panicked. "Someone could overhear, and that wouldn't be good for any of us. I know it's an inconvenience, but would you mind coming back to my room?"

Why did this feel like a trap? My gaze bounced around our suite. I desperately wished Benji were here with me.

If I could find him before meeting up with Bree, it would be two against one. And Benji was strong. A handyman. He knew how to use that strength. We'd be okay. Probably.

"Uh...yeah. Okay. We can be there in thirty minutes." Truthfully, it wouldn't take nearly that long, as long as Benji hadn't wandered too far. But I wanted to catch Bree by surprise, throw her off guard. If she was expecting us in thirty, but we arrived in ten, then we would have the upper hand.

Bree released what sounded like a sigh of relief. "Wonderful. I'll see you then."

My heart raced as I called Benji. It turned out that he was already on his way back up to our room, but my heart didn't slow down, even after he'd arrived.

"Bree asked us to come back up to her room," I said, the words bursting out.

I thought about telling him my fears that Bree was setting us up.

But I didn't. 'Cause that made me sound like a crazy person. And that was the last thing I needed right now.

"Is everything okay?" he asked, while holding something out to me.

A giant piece of cake sealed in plastic, like it had come out of a vending machine.

My mind went blank as I took it from him. It was beautiful. There was nothing in the world in that moment except for me and that cake. "Is that chocolate chip chocolate? It's huge."

Benji lifted a shoulder, like it wasn't a big deal, but his eyes were crinkled in amusement. "Turns out they have a cake machine downstairs. Fifteen different flavors. Figured you could use a pick-me-up."

Yes, I could. Unable to express how much the gesture meant to me, I leaped forward and wrapped my arms around Benji's neck. "Thank you," I whispered.

Benji laughed. "You're welcome. But you were saying something about needing to revisit Bree's room?"

Oh, yeah.

I stepped back. As much as I wanted to dig into that piece of chocolate cake, it was going to have to wait. I placed it on the desk next to me.

"She says there's something important she needs to tell us—something she kept from us earlier."

Benji didn't look thrilled at the news, but he extended his hand toward the door, indicating that he'd follow me out. Always the best friend—always my biggest supporter.

We rode the elevator down to the fifth floor and walked to room 529.

As I raised my hand to knock, a door across the hallway opened.

13

Elijah exited the room across the hall, patting his pockets and pulling down on his vest, as if he was making sure he looked as crisp and wrinkle-free as his job required.

The door shut behind him, and Elijah turned toward the elevator. His footsteps faltered when he noticed us, like he'd thought he was alone, but then his characteristic smile exploded over his features.

"If it isn't my two favorite guests," he said.

"Hello, Elijah," Benji said, returning the smile. "Do you ever stop working?"

Elijah paused and actually seemed to think about the answer to that question. I was impressed. Most people just said what they thought others wanted to hear, not bothering to really consider what they'd been asked.

"No, sir. I don't," he said. "The resort needs the help,

and I need the overtime. If we don't have guests who need help with their luggage, there are plenty of other ways I can be of service."

"You saving up for a new car? Maybe a big vacation?" I asked, curious. I'd always been fascinated by the type of people who chose to spend extra hours at work rather than relaxing in front of the TV at home. Usually, it took something big to drive that kind of motivation.

"Oh, no, ma'am," Elijah said with a quick shake of his head, as if he was offended by the thought. "My mother needs a medical treatment, and you won't find my stepfather helping out anytime soon." His words came to a sudden stop, and his lips clamped shut. Elijah seemed surprised at his openness, and embarrassed. "I'm sorry, I get carried away sometimes. But if there is anything I, or my colleagues, can help you with, please let us know. We want to make sure you have the nicest stay possible. You know, considering the circumstances."

And then he scurried away, like he couldn't get out of there fast enough.

"Poor guy," I said, watching as he disappeared into the elevator. "Working all these long hours so he can take care of his mother."

I pushed down any feelings of guilt and regret—I never would have done the same for my own mother at his age. I hoped I'd changed since then.

I turned my attention back to room 529 and raised my

hand to knock on Bree's door, but Benji caught my hand and pointed to his ear. I paused and listened.

Arguing.

"Mom, none of this was my fault," a voice said from inside the room.

"But to deceive everyone like that—it wasn't right."

A long sigh. "Mom, I'm not in the mood for this right now. Believe it or not, I am sorry that Mark is dead, and you barging in like this isn't helpful."

Looked like I wasn't the only one with mommy issues.

"Well, someone has to say it like it is. If you hadn't—"

Bree cut her mother off. "We're done talking about this. I'm expecting someone, and I don't want you here when they arrive."

"Fine. But this conversation isn't over. And if it's that detective again, you don't need to tell him anything. It's none of his business."

I took a step back, not wanting to be caught eavesdropping. "Maybe we should come back."

Without waiting for a response from Benji, I hurried back toward the elevator, pushing the UP button over and over, as if the elevator would recognize my urgency.

Benji threw an anxious glance toward Bree's room, then joined me. "Maybe it's not what it sounded like."

The elevator chimed and the door opened, but Bree's door opened at the same time, and I spun to face whoever was there, as if we'd just gotten off the elevator and hadn't overheard a thing.

A frowning middle-aged woman marched toward us, seemingly without any goodbyes for Bree. She spotted us, and her uneasy expression transformed into one of genuine surprise, which then morphed into a smile. She put on the air of someone who had hosted countless parties and had to look happy about it. I didn't doubt that her worst enemy could show up and she'd manage to mask every emotion with an air of hospitality and grace.

Now wasn't any different.

"Benji," she said with a smile that almost looked genuine. "My husband mentioned that he'd run into you earlier. I'm so happy to see you, even if it is under these circumstances. I'll bet your parents feel a bit less guilty about not being able to attend the wedding now that we're all being held captive."

Benji had the same air of hospitality as Mrs. Garrett as he returned her smile. "You'd think so, but they were actually disappointed they were missing out on all the excitement. Of course, I haven't had the chance to give them all the grisly details yet. I'm sure the folks back home will be able to manage that, though."

"Oh, yes. I remember the gossip in Amor. You can use it like currency there," Mrs. Garrett said, her expression darkening for the slightest of moments, and then her smile was back. "I understand that you are here to visit Bree, so don't let me keep you."

Mrs. Garrett took a step toward the elevator but then turned. "It's been a traumatic couple of days. Bree... She hasn't been quite herself. Prone to exaggerating. Be patient with her, will you? And don't take everything she says at face value. What she needs now more than anything is a friend. Nothing more."

Her gaze seemed to linger on me for those final words, and I swallowed hard, hoping I was misinterpreting the meaning behind that gaze.

That Bree didn't need anyone else investigating the death of her fiancé.

Even if inviting Benji and me up to her room was a trap, I needed now, more than ever, to hear what Bree had to tell us.

And contrary to what her mother had said, I intended on believing every word of it.

14

"I'm sorry to call you down here again," Bree said, then gestured toward the couch. "Please, sit down." Earlier when we'd visited, she'd seemed nervous, but more like she was anxious to get out of there and move on with her life.

It was different now. She practically radiated anxiety, her body unable to stay still. She paced the small room several times before allowing herself to sit on a chair across from us. And then she was up and pacing again.

"You all right?" I finally asked.

Bree seemed distracted, her attention scattered. This certainly wasn't a trap. But whatever information she might have for us was practically eating her from the inside.

"Why don't you join us?" I said, motioning to the chair she'd just vacated.

Bree's gaze finally settled on me, and her expression cleared. "Thank you." She gave a nervous laugh, then sat back down. "I just spoke with an old roommate of mine, told her about the canceled wedding. I didn't bring up the murder. Didn't think she needed to know about that." A pause. "She invited me out to California to stay with her for a bit. I think I'll take her up on it."

That was an interesting, and abrupt, change of topic. Especially because we knew she hadn't just gotten off the phone with an old friend. Maybe earlier she had. But that argument she'd had with her mother had nothing to do with California.

"That sounds lovely," I said, my voice weaker than I'd intended. I sucked in a quick breath and tried again. "I'm sure a change of scenery is just what you need."

Another pause.

"Is that why you called us up here?" Benji asked, his tone soft. He'd always had a gentle way with others that helped them lower their guard. And the funny thing was, he didn't even realize it. He would have made a great psychologist.

Bree started to nod, then hesitated, and it morphed into a shake of the head. "No, it's not. You see... Well, I know things that I shouldn't. I thought of telling the detective, but he seems to twist everything I say into something awful. Take earlier, for instance. He asked what my relationship was like with Mark. I told him that it wasn't great. That Mark wasn't a kind man. I was trying to keep things general, you know. He immediately jumped to the conclusion that I could have killed Mark to get out of an abusive relationship. Can you believe that?"

I swallowed hard, then gave Bree my most sympathetic expression, as if I hadn't jumped to the same exact conclusion.

"I tried explaining that Mark treated everyone terribly, not just me, and that I couldn't have possibly killed him, because I was down at the wedding. The detective didn't care. He claims he can't find me on a single security camera."

Now that I thought of it, Bree was right. She hadn't shown up a single time in all the security footage that Flash had sent me.

"You were at the wedding venue, though, weren't you?" I asked.

Bree nodded nervously. "Yes, but I had slipped into a seat in the back just as the wedding was starting because I didn't want my mother to realize that it was Melinda in the wedding dress, and not me. Didn't want Mark's parents to know either. Turns out that the seat I chose is the one blind spot of the entire place. Just my luck with how the last couple of days have gone for me."

"That's worse than bad luck," Benji said, releasing a heavy breath as he shook his head. "That's bad luck on a cosmic level."

"And the more I try to explain myself, the worse it

gets," Bree said. "I didn't kill Mark. I think I know who did, though."

I moved forward to the edge of the sofa, leaning forward.

"I think Mark's girlfriend did it," Bree said, her tone timid, like she thought she'd get in trouble just for voicing the thought. "Because he was going through with the wedding."

"She was here?" I asked, shocked that a man's mistress would have the audacity to show up at his wedding.

Bree's mother had told us not to take what Bree said at face value. Maybe this was what she was referring to.

"She had wanted Mark to break off our engagement, but he wouldn't hear of it," Bree said, looking anywhere except at us. Like she was embarrassed by what she had to say. "I wanted to tell all this to the detective, but everything I said seemed to convince him further that I did it. Blaming Mark's girlfriend wouldn't help things and would only come across as a last-ditch attempt to save myself. It's the same reason I didn't tell you—because it made me sound like a jealous fiancée who had a vendetta. I can't keep quiet anymore, though, Maddie. I really think she did it."

It was certainly possible. A jealous rage, perhaps. But I also could understand it from the detective's perspective and could construe it as misdirected blame.

"What makes you think she's guilty?" I asked, attempting to remain neutral and open to the idea.

"Remember how I said Mark had been cheating on me

with his dad's secretary?" Bree asked. "Well, the whole office was invited to the wedding. Business associates, clients, and that included the secretary. None of the other low-level employees bothered to make the trek out here—they would have had to cover their own expenses."

"But the secretary did."

Bree's lips pulled into a scowl. They seemed to do that whenever she thought of her ex-fiancé. "She didn't pay for anything—that was all Mark. He told his parents that he'd cover the expenses for his own room. They were thrilled, thinking he was finally interested in taking some responsibility for his life, but really, he just wanted to be able to get an adjoining room without them knowing."

It took a moment for my brain to catch up with everything. My gaze swung wildly around Bree's room. I'd assumed that when Elijah had said Mark had an adjoining room with his fiancée, he'd meant Bree. But the only door here that didn't lead to the hallway was the bathroom.

"He kept your room on one side, and hers on the other?" I asked, incredulous. And just when I thought my opinion of him couldn't get any worse. My thoughts jumped to the woman who'd recently lost her fiancé. "Does this secretary of his have a name?"

Even before she said a word, I already knew.

Amanda.

Images of a woman with red hair in a jade dress jumped to mind. A woman who had been arguing with Robert after the failed wedding.

It had been only a fleeting glance, and I hadn't recognized her in the restaurant. But it was all coming together.

It wasn't Bree who'd had access to Mark without leaving her room.

It was the secretary.

15

"I can't believe I felt sorry for Amanda," I said, anger coursing through me as we left Bree's room. "I mean, I'd thought it was strange that two women in the same hotel had lost their fiancés on the same weekend. But what kind of man proposes to multiple women? Not only that, but Amanda knew everything all along. Shared a room with him, even. On his wedding day."

The door across the hall opened, and I stopped talking just as Robert was stepping out.

"I thought I heard familiar voices," he said. "I've been meaning to stop by your room. How's the manhunt coming along?"

I was unsure how to answer that. Whatever was happening on the fifth floor of this resort, I wanted nothing to do with it. A murder had been quite enough, but now we had a loveless engagement, a woman taking her sister's place at the sister's wedding, and as it turned out, the groom had a second fiancée.

Never mind that both the father of the bride and the brother of the groom had asked me to find the killer.

"Just fine," I said, forcing a smile.

Relief passed over Robert's face. "That's wonderful to hear. So, you know who it is, then?" His gaze jumped to Bree's door, as if he expected us to announce that he'd been right all along and that Bree had indeed killed her fiancé.

I shared a look with Benji, but I couldn't decipher what his was trying to tell me. How much should I reveal to Robert? And how much did he already know? Surely he must have at least known that his brother was engaged to two women at the same time.

"Unfortunately, not yet," I said, turning back to Robert. I tried to look as disappointed as he did. "Much like a tangled ball of yarn, there is a lot to unravel, and I'm still uncertain how to find where it all begins. Maybe you could be of some help."

"Anything," Robert said. "I was just on my way down to dinner, if you'd like to join me."

I really didn't want to. I was tired of talking to people—questioning them. I just wanted a moonlit night at White Sands with a concert playing in front of me, and Benji beside me. Was a proper date too much to ask for? And not being accused of murder—or accusing others—while I was at it?

"I'm sorry, we have other plans," I said. "But I do have one question, if you don't mind."

"Of course." Robert smiled, like there was nothing he'd like more in the world that to help us in that moment.

"Were you as involved in your father's business pursuits as your brother was?"

Robert's smile momentarily dipped, but then it returned to its full wattage. "No. That was their thing that they enjoyed doing together. I chose another route."

He didn't expound on what that route may have been, and I had the feeling that I wasn't supposed to ask.

"It's interesting to hear you say that, because from what I understand, your father had no intention of bringing Mark over to his new venture."

Robert couldn't hide his surprise, and for a moment he was left without a reply. And, unless it was my imagination, Robert almost looked sad at this news. He blinked rapidly and shook his head.

"No, I didn't know. And I don't think Mark did either. He was counting on making the move with my father. They had worked together for years, but Mark's was a minor role compared to what he thought he was capable of. Or more accurately, what he felt he deserved. With my father and Mr. Garrett venturing out on their own, it could have been a big opportunity, career-wise, for Mark." Robert leaned against the wall, a look of contemplation crossing his handsome features. "I wonder why my father decided to cut him out of the new company."

"Maybe because he knew the type of man that Mark really was." As soon as I said it, I wished I could claw those words back. Even if it had been true, it had been insensitive. And certainly not something you'd say to a grieving family member. I was better than that.

But Robert didn't seem angry at my words. Instead, he gave a thoughtful nod, like the answer didn't surprise him and was instead expected.

"I think you might be right," he said. He was quiet for a moment, then seemed to shake himself from it. "Well, I better get downstairs. You'll let me know if you discover anything new, though, won't you?"

I didn't answer right away, not wanting to make any promises I couldn't keep, so Benji responded in my stead. "Of course."

Robert nodded to us in lieu of goodbyes, but I had a last parting thought as he walked toward the elevator. "Do you know if Amanda is in her room?"

"I saw her leave about an hour ago," Robert said over his shoulder. "Said something about an outdoor movie."

And then he disappeared into the open elevator.

So, Robert didn't work at his father's company, but he did know Amanda.

"He knows more than he's saying," I said.

Benji slipped his hand into mine, sending a thrill of both familiarity and attraction. "Of course he does. Even in death, he's protecting his brother's reputation. He's asked you to find his brother's killer and is willing to help, but that doesn't mean you need full access to all of Mark's dirty secrets to do it."

"My kids would never show that kind of loyalty," I said, pulling Benji after me. "In fact, I'm fairly certain that Lilly would create a blog dedicated to all her brother's misdeeds, and he in turn would hack it and turn it into a blog that told nothing but how heroic he was. Probably make himself into a spy or CIA agent or something."

Benji laughed. A sound that I'd been missing the past couple of days.

"Yes, that does sound like them," he said. "But they might also surprise you. Sure, they fight and pretend they can't stand each other, but if anyone threatened the other, I have no doubt that they'd protect each other fiercely. At all costs."

I knew Benji was right, and the fact that he knew my kids so well gave me comfort. "Thank you." I tilted my face up toward him. "For everything."

"Even this weekend?" he asked, his eyes lit up in the way they always did when he teased me.

"Yes, I think so," I said, surprising myself with the realization that I didn't regret coming. Even with everything going on.

"So, do you think the girlfriend did it? Or the second fiancée...whatever she is?"

I raised a shoulder. "I honestly have no idea. If she was jealous, why not kill Bree instead of Mark?"

"Maybe because Mark did something that made her

angry." He gave me a pointed look. "Like committing to marry another woman."

"I'm serious," I said. Nothing about this situation made sense to me. But maybe some of the answers we were looking for would be at that evening's outdoor movie. "You in the mood for a comedy?"

WHEN WE ARRIVED at the large screen that had been erected sometime since we'd last been outside, we discovered that there was indeed going to be an outdoor movie, but it didn't start until eight o'clock, and it was only six-thirty now.

And yet, Robert had said that Amanda had left an hour earlier for the outdoor movie. She wasn't here—no one was. And she wouldn't be for quite some time.

So, where was she?

"Maybe she went to the concert at White Sands instead," I said, but I already saw the faulty logic in my statement.

"The outdoor movie doesn't start until eight o'clock because that's when it's dark enough. Same with the full moon concert," Benji pointed out.

Yup. That was the faulty logic.

I didn't have a better suggestion, though. "So, what do we do?"

Benji was saved from answering when a high-pitched shriek pierced the night. "I didn't do it."

He and I spun toward the sound and were met with two police officers escorting a handcuffed Amanda through the resort grounds. "Sure you didn't," one of them grumbled.

Amanda spotted us as they walked past. "Tell them I didn't do it," she pleaded, though she had no reason to believe we knew what she was talking about, let alone that she was innocent.

But in that moment, I believed her. As a psychologist, I'd had a lot of people lie to me. I'd also had a lot of people tell me what they thought I wanted to hear. But the fear in her eyes—the confusion—it was all genuine.

Of course, I'd be afraid if I'd been arrested for murder too.

Especially if I'd done it.

16

"Detective Holbrook, are you certain that Amanda is the one who did it?" Never mind that I'd been convinced of it myself not long ago.

The detective sat in the same chair he'd questioned me from that morning. He studied me, leaning back and placing his hands on his stomach. I sat alone and uncomfortable under his gaze. Benji had chosen not to come with me, saying he thought the detective might be more forthcoming if he wasn't there. Benji could have been right, but that didn't stop me from missing his reassuring presence.

"Are you saying you'd rather I keep you on my suspect list?" Detective Holbrook asked.

"No, of course not. But I'm just not sure you have the right person. Amanda loved Mark. They were engaged to be married."

I had expected Detective Holbrook to be surprised by this revelation, but he merely nodded. "Yes, they were. Mark even booked them adjoining rooms. And then he rescinded the offer of matrimony yesterday afternoon, right before his other wedding was set to happen. Told her that he was choosing Bree and that whatever he'd had with Amanda was over."

I tried to not look as surprised as I felt. Amanda had still been wearing her engagement ring when we'd met her at lunch. I'd have thought he'd take back the ring at the same time he broke things off.

"And you think his murder was a spur-of-the-moment thing. An act of passion," I guessed.

"That's what it looks like." The detective saw the uncertainty in my expression, and he released an impatient sigh. "What is it?"

"It's just that if it was a crime of passion, how did Amanda get the cake knife? It had been downstairs at the wedding venue. She would have had to come all the way downstairs, grab it, take it back up to the fifth floor to kill him with it, then return the cake knife downstairs. And then she'd have had to move the body all the way out to the dunes and bury it. You looked at the security footage. Did anything suggest she did that?"

The detective shifted uncomfortably in his chair. "Frankly, it's none of your business."

"You're okay with arresting anybody, then, whether they did it or not. As long as it allows you to claim another victory and move on to the next case. Is that the kind of office this is?"

I knew I was pushing it, but I was so tired of all of this. And I really did want to know if that was the kind of office the detective was running, because if it was, nothing I did would make any difference and I might as well go out and enjoy what was left of my weekend with Benji.

Detective Holbrook seemed taken aback by my outburst. "You, of all people, should know that isn't what is happening here," he said, taking on a defensive tone. "I have scoured those videos and interviewed nearly two hundred people in the past two days. And for you to accuse me of—"

His words broke off, and I immediately knew I'd gone too far.

"I'm sorry," I quickly said. And I hoped he heard how much I meant it. Fatigue and frustration had set in, and I was taking it out on him. "I know you are doing your best. That was unfair of me." I paused. "Ever since you accused me of killing Mark, I've been doing everything I can to figure out what could have happened. And I've run into all the dead ends you have. I understand how you must feel."

Detective Holbrook was already shaking his head before I'd finished speaking. "You can't possibly know how I feel. My job is on the line. Innocent lives are at stake. You —" He seemed to be trying to find the right words. "You dress up and play detective, then go home, however it turns out. So you need to trust me when I say, it is not the same thing."

That was a valid point.

"So...I really am off the suspect list, then?"

Detective Holbrook hesitated, as if determining how much he should say. "I wouldn't go so far as to say that. But Amanda had the means—adjoining rooms. And certainly motive. The way we figure it, she took the cake knife before guests started arriving for the wedding—we do have her on camera thirty minutes before it began. After killing Mark, she waited for just the right moment to return the knife. Probably when all the chaos broke out when he didn't show up for the wedding. And as far as motive goes, it's self-explanatory."

"That's not an act of passion," I said. "And I still don't think she did it. How did she move the body without anybody noticing?"

Detective Holbrook opened his mouth to speak, then seemed to change his mind and closed it again. "She must have tossed him over the balcony, then drove him out to White Sands on one of the golf carts," he finally said, though his words lacked conviction. "We have her leaving and returning to her room several times during the period when she was supposed to be down at the wedding."

As illogical as everything sounded when Detective Holbrook laid out his reasoning, Amanda didn't have an alibi. She couldn't claim to have been at the wedding. That wasn't good.

"Can I speak to her?" I asked.

The detective straightened, like he was ready to take back this conversation, and the investigation, and shook his head. "Impossible. I'm not finished interrogating her, and once I am, she'll be transferred to the local jail while we take care of the paperwork."

"Oh, come on, it couldn't hurt," I said. "Besides, it would look good if your decision was corroborated by a well-known psychologist."

That last part was a bit of a stretch.

"Amanda's arrest is based on evidence and probable cause. I don't need a psychologist to tell my boss I did a good job," Detective Holbrook said, bristling.

Maybe Benji should have sat in on this one. I had thought I was forming a connection with the detective, but I'd lost him somewhere along the way.

"I know you don't. All I meant was—"

The detective raised a hand in a motion that told me I could see my way out. "It's all been taken care of, Ms. Swallows. Have a lovely evening, and enjoy the fact that you aren't being arrested."

"You never had any evidence on me," I said. Other than my prints on the cake knife.

Detective Holbrook didn't respond, and I determined that our conversation was officially finished.

"Well?" Benji asked as soon as I'd left.

I glanced back at the security office. "We really need to speak with Amanda, and he's stonewalling me. Won't let me get anywhere near her. At this point, I doubt I could get as far as the security office. Amanda wasn't at the wedding, but it would have been difficult for her to pull off this thing alone."

"You think she was working with someone."

I hesitated. "I don't know."

"You do have a connection who might be able to help, you know."

Benji was looking at me like the answer was obvious when it was anything but.

"Go on," I said.

"Sheriff Potts is responsible for the entire county, right?"

I nodded slowly, thinking I knew where he was going with this. I'd managed to establish a working relationship with our hometown sheriff, and I'd been able to go to her for help in the past. And vice versa. "Yeah, sure. But is this resort even in the same county as Amor? I know counties are big, but they aren't that big, are they?"

"No clue," Benji said. "But even if it's not, Sheriff Potts still has connections, right?"

"I suppose. It might be worth a shot."

"Think she'll be glad to hear from you?" he asked as I moved to a quiet corner of the long hallway where I was least likely to be overheard.

"Not a chance."

. . .

"I HEARD you'd gotten yourself into another mess," Sheriff Potts said the moment she answered. No *Hello* or *How are you*? "What is it you need?"

The fact that she was offering help was at least promising.

"I need to talk to someone Detective Holbrook arrested, but he won't let me anywhere near her."

The sheriff snort-laughed. "Of course he won't. You're not a lawyer or a family member. He can't just allow random people to speak with prisoners. At the jail, there are visiting hours. You can go then."

Or maybe she wasn't offering to help.

"You allowed me to talk to Andy when he was arrested at the hot air balloon festival."

Silence. And not the good kind.

"I did what I thought was right in the moment. And if you keep bringing up things like that, you won't talk to that prisoner, or any other, ever again," Sheriff Potts said, her tone an angry whisper. "I made an exception for you, but you can't expect that of others. If anything were to go wrong, he could lose his job, and he's not going to take that risk so that a nosy psychologist can go talk to a murder suspect. Especially when the psychologist was suspected of the same murder."

I didn't know what to say to that. I knew Sheriff Potts had bent rules for me from time to time, but I hadn't stopped to think about the repercussions. That I had literally been asking the sheriff to put her job on the line for me.

"I'm sorry. I should have realized, and I didn't," I said. "I won't ask again. Promise."

And then I hung up, shame and embarrassment hanging over me.

Benji misunderstood my dark mood and put an arm around me. "She'll come through. She always does."

"No, not this time," I said, my voice quiet. "Maybe we should drop this one. Amanda does look good for the murder, and the detective will do his due diligence."

"You really believe that?" Benji asked, an eyebrow raised.

I shrugged. Because no, I didn't. But Benji had been right. Since I'd returned to my hometown two years earlier, our relationship had been founded on chasing after suspected murderers. And if we were going to have any chance at all of making this thing work, I had to stay in my lane. Do the job I was good at. And let law enforcement do theirs. I wasn't going to be responsible for anyone losing their job because I'd thought I could do it better.

"I think I'm done," I said, my voice small. "For good. I'm hanging up my detective hat and focusing on the things that matter." I held his gaze so he'd understand that he was one of those things.

Benji didn't look away.

"Sheriff Potts must have really done a number on you this time," he said. "I've never seen you back down like this. Not until you were absolutely certain that the police hadn't made a mistake."

Annoyance rose in my chest. I'd been accused of a lot of things, but being a quitter wasn't one of them. "I'm not backing down. I'm doing the right thing."

"Tomayto, tomahto."

That was when I heard my name being called from further down the hallway. Detective Holbrook was hurrying toward us, waving us down.

"Ms. Swallows, I'm glad I caught you before you got too far. If you'll follow me, you can see Amanda now."

I shared a surprised look with Benji. He was watching me, like he was wondering what I was going to do. I had just sworn off this investigation, after all.

Looked like Sheriff Potts had come through for me. And I wasn't about to let her risking her career go to waste.

"Of course, Detective. I appreciate you reconsidering."

He'd already turned back toward the security office without waiting for an answer, and I hurried after him, doing a victory dance all the way.

Maddie Swallows was back in business.

17

The room Amanda was being held in looked like any other office, albeit a bit sparse with the furniture. A small table. Two chairs.

As soon as the door thudded shut and I was finally alone with her, I realized I had no idea what I was doing there. I was grateful to Sheriff Potts for getting me this interview, but part of me wondered if I was just there to ease my conscience, considering that Amanda's arrest meant I would be able to return home the next day, no cloud over my head. No fear that someone would knock on my front door and say they'd changed their mind and decided to arrest me.

I wanted proof that she wasn't just a scapegoat.

I wanted proof that she was guilty.

"I didn't do what they are saying I did," Amanda said,

breaking the silence. Moisture gathered in her eyes, and I immediately felt bad for hoping it really was her that had killed Mark.

But even guilty people knew how to cry. They knew how to tug on people's heartstrings. Get people to doubt the facts that were as clear as day.

Then again, the same thing could be said about me or Bree. It was my fingerprints on the murder weapon. It was me who had discovered the body. And it was Bree who had every reason to want to kill the man.

And yet it was Amanda who was going to jail.

"You weren't at the wedding," I said, my voice soft. "And you had an adjoining room with Mark."

She sniffled as she sat down across the table from me. "I wasn't at the wedding because I couldn't bear to see him marry that ridiculous woman. It wasn't Bree that he loved. It was me. But she had the family connections, and I was destined to be the woman on the side. I was expected to be at the wedding, considering I've been his father's secretary for six years now. Thought I could handle it. I'd be sharing a connecting room with Mark, after all. I could pretend it was a romantic getaway for us, rather than what it truly was. Turned out I was wrong."

Amanda held up the finger that still held the large ring I'd noticed when we'd first met. "He proposed to me. Said it might take a couple of years to get things in order. But Mark promised that once he was established at his father's company, he would end the marriage with Bree and we'd finally get the life we'd been wanting."

Empty promises.

"Are you transferring to the new company with Mr. Peters?" I watched Amanda's expression closely.

Her lips twitched up into a small smile. "I am." She seemed very proud of this fact.

"And you didn't know that Mr. Peters had no intention of Mark also joining him?"

That had the desired effect. Amanda's gaze immediately hardened, and it seemed to take quite a bit of effort for her to soften it. "I wasn't privy to those types of things."

I knew for a fact that was a lie. The way Amanda wouldn't look at me. The way her hands were fidgeting with each other.

"You don't seem surprised."

Amanda hesitated, looked around the small room she was being held in, and then released a long sigh. "Guess it doesn't matter now. But yes, I had heard rumors. Once, when I was taking notes during a meeting, Mr. Garrett started to speak about it, but Mr. Peters quickly put a stop to that. I think he suspected that something was happening between myself and Mark. I don't think he wanted me running back to Mark and telling him what I had overheard."

"So, Mark promised to divorce Bree and marry you when he got a position at the new company. But he wasn't getting the job. So where did that leave you? Or maybe that was why you didn't attend the wedding downstairs—because you knew he would never marry you."

Amanda's eyes flashed. "I told him that he needed to choose her or me." Her voice hitched. "He chose her."

"This wouldn't by any chance be the reason he was sitting in the hallway right before the wedding, drunk, would it?"

Amanda lifted a shoulder. "Yeah. So what, we argued. And neither of us made it down to the wedding. It doesn't mean that I killed him."

"But you did have access to his room, and you did leave yours several times during the timeframe when he was murdered."

Amanda slumped back into her chair. "I'm telling you, I didn't kill him. Didn't even go into his room. I was too angry. I did leave a couple of times. Once was when Robert texted me, asking if I knew where Mark was. He was the only person Mark had confided in about us. I told him that the wedding had been postponed and Mark was in his room. When I discovered the wedding hadn't in fact been delayed, I went downstairs to find out what was going on. I was hoping that Mark had just told me it was postponed so he could get out of the wedding. Maybe he had changed his mind about marrying Bree."

That must have been when the detective had said Amanda had been on the security video before the wedding.

"I saw you and Robert talking. After the wedding had been canceled and guests were leaving."

Amanda nodded. "Yes, it was about an hour later. I'd knocked on Mark's door, asking him to let me in. There was no answer, and it was locked. I'd gone back downstairs, upset that he was refusing to talk to me. I wanted to work things out—fix things. And he wasn't even giving me the chance." She pulled up in a shuddered breath. "Now I realize that he was probably already dead at that point."

"That must be difficult for you, knowing that you were right next door when he was killed." I knew I was pushing it with that one. Knew it would probably cause her to shut me out. But I had to dig deep, and quickly. I had no idea how long I had before the detective would tell me that my time was up.

Amanda didn't get angry, though. Or shut me out. Instead, she cried. And continued crying. So much so that she couldn't speak.

If she was acting, this was a professional job.

"You don't know how many times I've thought, if only I hadn't started that argument," she finally said between sobs. "Maybe I'd have been there with him. Maybe I could have prevented it from happening."

I gave her my best sympathetic smile and waited for her breaths to even out a bit before I continued. "Surely you must have heard something, though. A yell. A thud. The killer moved Mark all the way out to White Sands, and they couldn't have kept something like that quiet."

"Like I told the detective, I didn't hear anything," Amanda yelled, switching abruptly from heartbroken to angry. She jumped from her chair. "I went downstairs to see if the wedding had really been postponed. I came back up, and thirty minutes later I have a baggage guy knocking on my door, seeing if I need anything. Then I hear him knocking on Mark's door. The door opens, I hear the guy asking Mark the same question. A few minutes later, the guy leaves."

That would have been around the time that the detective had received the call about the murder and housekeeping was going around, checking to make sure everything was all right.

"Of course, when *I* try talking to Mark, he doesn't answer the door," Amanda continued. "Gives me the cold shoulder. And then I went downstairs to see if Robert could talk some sense into him. End of story. After my argument with Mark, I never saw him again."

And then the tears returned.

I had a feeling I'd gotten everything Amanda was going to be able to tell me, but I thought I'd give one last effort.

"Do you know of anyone who might want to hurt him?" I asked.

Amanda snorted as she wiped at her tears. "You mean, other than everyone? As much as I loved Mark, I wasn't blind to his faults. And he had a lot of them. He was domineering and rude and driven, which was what made him so good at business. He was also infuriating. I don't think anyone at the office liked him—saw him as the boss's spoiled son who expected everything to be handed to him. Robert was the one that everyone liked."

Amanda abruptly stopped speaking, like our conversation had drained all the energy out of her.

"I appreciate you speaking with me," I said. Part of me felt like I was supposed to reassure Amanda and tell her it was all going to be okay. But I didn't know that it would be. I felt like I knew less now than when I'd first spoken with the detective that morning.

Amanda gave a slight nod but stopped me as I was slinging my purse over my shoulder. "You'll find who really did this, won't you? I know Robert asked you to help. He said you're the best."

I intended to tell her that I didn't know if I'd be able to prove who had killed Mark. That I wasn't a real detective. Usually when people asked for my help in this sort of thing, that was the line I gave them. Partially because it was true. But I also tended to use it as an excuse.

Because I was scared that I was going to let someone down, and that an innocent person was going to be punished for something they hadn't done.

I wasn't convinced of Amanda's innocence, despite the tears and the sincere gaze that had settled on me in that moment. But I also couldn't leave her with no hope.

Just in case Detective Holbrook was wrong about her.

"I'll do my best," I told her with a small smile.

As I left the security office, Detective Holbrook glanced

up from where he was working on paperwork at his desk. "Hope you enjoyed your field trip," he said with a grunt. "You didn't get anything she hasn't already told us."

Maybe not.

But there had to be something useful from what she'd told me. I just had to figure out what.

18

"Now what?" Benji asked. He sat next to me in the hotel lobby, dwarfed by their oversized chairs.

After leaving the security office, I didn't have it in me to return to our room on the ninth floor. What would be the point? I'd just worry, then have a new idea, then leave again. I'd lost count of how many times we'd been on the elevator.

"When employees checked all the rooms, they didn't report anything unusual, correct?"

Benji nodded. "Correct."

"And yet they were responding to an anonymous call that someone had been murdered."

I was talking to myself at this point, but I tended to do that when I was trying to figure out a complex problem. "Why did someone bother reporting the murder if they weren't going to tell the police where the body was? And if it had, in fact, been Amanda who killed Mark, she would have to have been working with someone. It was a man who made the anonymous call. And I don't buy the idea that Amanda was capable of lifting Mark and throwing him over the edge of the balcony onto a golf cart."

"Neither do I, but why wouldn't she tell the police she was working with someone? She's about to be transferred to a jail cell, and something tells me she's not the kind of woman who will do well there."

"There has to be someone, or something, we're over-looking." I attempted to stand from the overstuffed chair, forgetting the last time I'd tried getting out of one. I gave Benji a pleading look, and one side of his lips quirked up as he stood and held out a hand to help me.

I had just gotten to my feet when my gaze landed on a man who was walking briskly down the hallway. I recognized that scowl.

"What if we've been looking in the wrong direction and it didn't have anything to do with bitter fiancées? What if instead it had something to do with this business stuff their families are involved with?" I asked, an idea forming. "Most of the guests were business associates. There had to be people who weren't happy about Mr. Peters and Mr. Garrett breaking off to do their own thing. They'd probably be taking loyal clients with them, as well as some employees."

"Yeah, sure, that makes sense." Benji looked as if he

was trying to be supportive, but I could tell he wasn't thrilled at the prospect of chasing down a new lead.

"Just hear me out. When I got off on the wrong floor—when I first met Mark—there was another man who was just getting on the elevator, and he looked angry about something. I didn't think much of it at the time because I was in a hurry to get to the wedding. But in the security footage, I saw that he'd been arguing with Mark. I'd bet anything he was a co-worker or business associate of some kind."

And it was the same man who had just disappeared around the corner.

Without a word of warning for Benji, I began walking in the same direction, my strides long. I had to catch up with him.

"Where are we going?" Benji asked, his steps quick as he tried to keep up with me.

"To talk to that man." I didn't know what I would say. Accosting strangers wasn't my area of expertise. But I didn't know what else to do.

You could just trust the detective and assume that if Amanda isn't guilty, he'll figure it out, a small voice said in my head.

Yes, I could. It would be easier. I'd finally enjoy my weekend away with Benji. We could even go to the full moon concert.

The only problem was that I believed Amanda.

Maybe I was gullible, but I'd rather think of myself as intuitive.

"Who is he?" Benji asked.

"No idea."

A pause.

"So...we're chasing him for the entertainment factor?"

My lips twitched up at the edges, and I glanced over my shoulder. "You know me so well."

We rounded the hallway's corner and nearly ran over the mysterious man. He was standing at a vending machine, seemingly trying to decide between a candy bar and a pack of gum.

"Oh, I'm so sorry," I said, managing to regain my balance at the last second and avoid a disastrous collision.

The man grunted.

I pressed ahead anyway. "I'm Maddie, and this is Benji."

The man didn't answer, his attention solely focused on the vending machine, as though if he concentrated on it hard enough, Benji and I would disappear.

"Hi," Benji added with a little wave, though he looked like he'd rather be anywhere than trying to talk to a man who clearly wanted nothing to do with us.

But I would not be deterred. It wasn't like murderers were all happy and wanting to chat. If I were a murderer, I'd try to avoid conversation as much as possible too. Which was why we needed to have one. "You're here for Bree and Mark's wedding, aren't you?" I paused. "Or you were. Us too. Crazy situation, huh? Can't wait until they finally let us leave. Are you staying on the fifth floor where everything happened? That would be terrifying."

The man turned abruptly, his eyebrows furrowed so intensely that they met in the middle. "No, I'm on the second floor. Now, do you mind? I'd like to finish the rest of this disastrous weekend in peace, and you aren't helping."

I raised a questioning eyebrow. If he was staying on the second floor, what had he been doing on the fifth floor right before the wedding?

The man gave me a side glance and must have noticed my skepticism, and his scowl deepened. "I'll try a different vending machine."

He turned to leave, and without thinking, I stepped in his way. If I didn't talk to this guy now, he would disappear, and I wouldn't get another chance.

"Yesterday, I was getting off the elevator on the fifth floor as you were getting on. Seemed like you were pretty upset at someone. By the looks of things, that guy was Mark." My current approach was so direct that it bordered on rude, but I didn't know how else to proceed with this guy. He wasn't interested in chit chat, and I was counting the fact that I had gotten him to respond at all as a personal victory.

The man straightened to the point that he towered over us. I had seriously underestimated how big this guy was and was now questioning my tactic. "Did I look similar to the way I do now?" He gestured toward his angry expression.

I gave a little nod.

"And you're snooping around, asking questions because you think of yourself as a detective, right? Think you can help the police. Only problem is, if you think I killed him, what position does that put you in now? Who says I'd stop at Mark?"

Benji grabbed my arm, and I took a step back, following his lead.

"I was only concerned you might have come into contact with his killer, but it is clear that you are able to take care of yourself. So we'll get out of your hair now."

"Why?" the man said, his scowl still firmly in place. "So you can run and tell the detective that you found Mark's killer and he can come around knocking on my door again, bothering me?"

That hadn't been my intention, but now that he mentioned it, it might not be a bad idea to ask the detective if this guy was on his radar. Which would be difficult, considering we still didn't know his name. But we did know he was staying on the second floor.

"I'm sorry. You're right," I said, my voice soft. "We just want to help." It was very possible this man had killed Mark; he certainly had the temperament for it. But clearly I hadn't thought this through and I needed to brush up on my interrogation techniques. I crossed *accost suspect at vending machine* off my mental checklist. Both because it had been ineffective and also because if this man really was innocent, then I'd just made his bad day even worse.

I touched Benji's elbow and nodded toward the direction we'd come from. I was done. I sincerely hoped that Amanda was the killer because that was who the police would be transferring to their jail cell.

And I wasn't going to be standing in their way.

But then the man surprised me. "Wait." A long sigh. "It's pointless, but I can think of at least a dozen people at work who would have liked to take Mark out. And all of them are here right now."

I turned back, a mixture of curiosity and anger rushing through me. "Why would that be pointless?"

He raised a shoulder. "Because none of them would ever admit to it, and these guys are as corrupt as they come. Good at covering their tracks. It's the reason Mr. Peters is leaving with Mr. Garrett. They didn't like the direction our company has been going in the past few years and wanted to start something new—something honest."

I tried to keep my voice level as I said, "You know they're holding someone for his murder, don't you? She could be innocent."

The man nodded. "Yeah. Amanda. It's a shame too. Nice girl."

"And you're willing to stand by and let her take the fall for one of these other guys?"

He hesitated. "I keep my head down and do what

needs to be done. If I don't bother them, they don't bother me. And trust me when I say that these guys aren't the type whose radar I want to be on. If they forget I exist, all the better."

"Was Mark one of those guys? Is that why his dad wasn't taking him over to the new company?"

The man snorted. "Mr. Peters was finally putting his foot down, huh? Good for him." He gave an amused sort of chuckle. "Mark wasn't one of anybody. He thought himself above everyone else. Boss's son gets to walk around with his nose so high, he can pretend no one else exists, right?"

"So...not a team player."

The man outright laughed at that. "He wasn't important enough to be on a team. Mark was a glorified errand boy. Mr. Peters didn't trust him with anything more than that. And golf. He had a way of connecting to potential clients on the range, so I suppose he was good for something. Not valuable enough for the new company, though, it seems."

The man seemed to be loosening up now, eager to tell us what a terrible person Mark had been. Maybe he hadn't wanted to speak ill of the dead, but he was plenty willing now.

"I didn't catch your name," I ventured, hoping he trusted us enough for at least that.

It seemed the man didn't see any harm in it, because he answered after only a brief pause. "I'm Kent. I work in marketing. Between you and me, it wouldn't matter if I had the most amazing advertising campaign in the world. Nothing is saving that sinking ship, and Mr. Peters and Mr. Garrett leaving the company is them saving themselves. The fact that they weren't bringing Mark over means that they were leaving him to drown."

That was an interesting analogy.

"Looks like you saw the writing on the wall," I said. "Are you jumping ship as well?"

"Hoping to. I thought it would look good if the boss saw me at the wedding. Thought I'd get the chance to say hi, maybe see if they have room for me at the new company. I saw it as my way in. That was why I was on the fifth floor yesterday, visiting Mark. I was asking if he could put in a good word for me, you know, before I approached his dad. Thought maybe he could soften him up for me. I should have known he'd turn me down, but I'd helped him out the previous month with something that had made him look good and thought I'd take my chances."

Okay, so the company was doing poorly, and everyone was going to be left behind, except for those that Mr. Peters and Mr. Garrett thought important enough to bring along. Which didn't include Mr. Peters' own son. But that information wasn't particularly new, or useful.

"You say that no one liked Mark and he wasn't important enough to even be on a team at work. Seems like he was a floater, just trying to ride on his daddy's coattails. But why would you think that's motive for murder? If everyone

murdered co-workers they didn't get along with, compa-
nies couldn't function."

Kent smirked, as if he couldn't wait to reveal what he
knew, which was a far cry from the man we'd met just
minutes earlier. "That's probably because most people
don't threaten their co-workers so they'll give you credit for
stuff you didn't do."

"In what way would he threaten them?" I didn't mean
to sound so skeptical, but it did sound a bit far-fetched.
The boss's son thought he was better than everyone else
but stole credit for work they'd done? Thinking back to
Mark in the hallway, and how he had wanted to use Bree
to help solidify his place at the new company, made me
stop and realize that yes, it was exactly the kind of thing
that Mark would have done.

"Threatening that he'd get them fired and stuff like
that. It's not crazy, and if you've done any research at all,
you know it," Kent said.

"But they had dirt on him that they could have used in
retaliation, right? You guys had to have known that he was
cheating on his fiancée with Amanda."

Kent's expression clouded. "I didn't know until just
recently. I hate that she got mixed up with a guy like that.
She should have known something like this would
happen."

I balked, and Benji placed a hand on my lower back,
reminding me to remain calm. His touch could always do
that for me. I didn't speak until I thought I could keep my

voice steady. "You're telling me that she should have known her boyfriend would be murdered right before marrying his fiancée, and that it would be blamed on her?"

Kent didn't smile as he nodded, his expression serious. "Yes. With that family, that is exactly what she should have expected."

"That seems a little dramatic," I said. "The rest of the family seems decent enough."

Kent laughed, but it lacked any humor. "Mark wasn't even the worst of them."

"Who could be worse than Mark?"

Kent turned his attention back to the vending machine, finally deciding on the pack of gum. "His brother, Robert."

19

I felt sick. How could I not have seen it? Robert arguing with Amanda. Randomly showing up at our hotel room, begging us to find Mark's killer. His hotel room was across the hall from Mark's, so he certainly had easy access to his brother.

I'd protested at first. Robert had said he didn't even work with his dad. Which was technically true. He was a lawyer who did a lot of contract work. And one of his biggest clients?

The company that his father and brother worked for.

He'd bent the truth like a master manipulator.

"We have to warn people," I said. "We can start with the detective and work our way from there."

My steps were quick as I hurried back toward the lobby.

"Do you have to run?" Benji asked, his long legs easily

matching my stride. "I've gotten more exercise this weekend trying to keep up with you than I've had in the past six months."

"Considering we were just told that there is a very dangerous man on the loose who no one even remotely suspects, yes, I do need to run."

Kent hadn't seemed as convinced that Robert had killed his brother. Even though he'd just told us that Robert was far worse than Mark, he'd insisted he still felt that someone at work had done it. Said he thought the co-workers had more at stake. But Kent only knew what he had observed at work and the gossip that was passed around when people got bored.

If being a psychologist had taught me anything, it was that family issues ran deep and something that had been buried decades earlier could suddenly detonate, like a land mine that had been long forgotten.

And it didn't usually take much.

We reached the security office in record time, and I barged into the office without knocking. I didn't have time for silly stuff like protocol.

"Detective, I missed something. I'm so sorry, but I know who it was. You need to find—"

I wished I had knocked.

Because sitting across from the detective was none other Robert.

They both looked up, surprise etched across their features.

Once the shock of the moment passed, the detective settled into a look of fury.

Robert, on the other hand, had an expression that held curious amusement. Like he was wondering how much I knew. And that no matter what I thought had happened, I'd never be able to prove it.

"This is the last straw, Ms. Swallows," Detective Holbrook spat out. "I have put up with your questions and your lack of respect far too long. If I see you in my office one more time, I am arresting you for obstruction of justice."

"But—"

The detective gave his head a vigorous shake. "No. This is it. Amanda is being transferred in an hour, and you are going home first thing tomorrow. If you are disappointed that the attention is no longer on you, I can arrange for you to get all the attention you need. In a courtroom."

"If you are so certain you've arrested the correct person, then why is he here?" I asked, pointing to Robert. Normally I would say a person should be careful in a situation like this, but all common sense had flown out the window and I was going on pure impulse.

I didn't know why I expected the detective to actually give me a straight answer.

Instead, his face turned a frightening shade of purple, and he ordered me out of the office. It wasn't until he pulled the handcuffs out that I realized just how serious he was.

On my way out the door, I was tempted to shout at the detective, proclaiming Robert's guilt. But by the time I determined to do so, the door had been slammed in my face, and I was left on the other side of it.

"Well, that was completely uncalled for," I said, staring at the door. Benji had had the good sense to stay outside the office, and he gave me a patient smile.

"Even if Robert did it, storming the castle isn't going to do much good. Not if we don't have anything more to go on than the fact that a man at a vending machine told us that Robert is ten times worse than his brother. Which, if we had known he was a lawyer, we may have been able to surmise." He waited a beat, as if expecting at least a smile for his lawyer joke, but I was too worked up to offer one. When Benji didn't receive so much as a courtesy laugh, he lifted a shoulder. "We need proof. Without it, there's no point in going to Detective Holbrook. You'd just be asking for him to arrest you."

I hated that Benji was right.

"How on earth are we supposed to get proof?" I asked, my heart falling. "Everyone Robert argued with is either dead or being held by the police. Not only that, but we don't even have a motive."

Benji nodded slowly. "Yes, that is a problem." He paused. "Maybe we can find someone who can place him at White Sands National Park yesterday afternoon. That would at least give us something to go on. We could see if he rented a golf cart or a sled or something."

My heart picked itself back up, and I leaped forward, wrapping my arms around Benji's neck. "You are a genius."

He placed his hands on my waist and grinned. "I do what I can."

"Well, you should do it more often. Maybe then I could get a break from fighting crime once in a while."

Benji gave an exaggerated shudder. "Thanks, but no thanks. I get it enough just being friends with you. I don't need any more drama in my life."

Friends. The way the word rolled so easily off his tongue...the way it always had. It left bitter disappointment in its wake. But I didn't have time to psychoanalyze what it meant right then, because we had a killer to catch. It turned out that the investigation was far from over.

Next stop, the golf shop.

"You're sure Robert Peters didn't rent a sled yesterday?" I asked for the third time. They had no record of him taking out a sled or a golf cart, and I doubted the answer would change if I asked for a fourth time.

"A receipt is needed for every expenditure," Benji added. "Company policy. And I never received a receipt." His voice had taken on an official tone, implying that he had every right to the information. It wasn't lying, technically, since he'd never claimed to be Robert. And he was correct in saying that he'd never received a receipt when we'd rented our own sled.

"Sorry," the woman behind the counter said. She didn't look sorry, more like she was hoping we'd leave soon. Understandable. I'd want us to leave too.

"Thanks anyway," Benji said, and he led me out of the shop.

"Well, that was a complete waste of time," I said, pouting in frustration. I knew that I looked like a three-year-old, but I couldn't help it. In the past, when I'd ended up in situations where murderers were running loose, I'd had my kids. Last time I'd even had my mom. My kids had skills that I didn't, and, because they were teenagers, they were able to get away with more than I was.

But I didn't have my support system here. My team. And this whole trip had been nothing but roadblock after roadblock after roadblock.

"It wasn't a complete waste," Benji said. "Now we know that he wasn't the one who buried Mark out at White Sands. That has to count for something."

"I guess. But I really thought he'd done it."

Benji gave a thoughtful nod. "I did too. But just because we don't have the evidence doesn't mean he's off the hook. Who would know more about Robert and Mark's relationship? Someone who could give us the motive."

"Amanda, but there's no way we're getting in to talk to her anytime soon."

"That is a very true statement. Who else?"

I could tell Benji had someone in mind, but he wanted

me to figure it out for myself. Maybe he wanted me to feel like I was useful so I'd stop pouting. "His parents."

Benji nodded. "True, but I doubt we'll get anything from them. They have no reason to trust us, and no parent is going to throw their son under the bus."

"Even if he killed their other son?" I asked.

"Even then. Because they won't want to believe it's true."

Realization dawned. "But someone who was close to the family who has no qualms with saying how much he disliked Mark could be useful. Like say, Mr. Garrett?"

"Exactly." Benji grinned, like he was proud of me for finally getting there, and I was slightly embarrassed that it had taken me so long.

My thoughts jumped to the argument we'd overheard between Bree and her mother. "Maybe we should invite him down here to take a walk around the resort grounds. You know, just in case there are listening ears that we'd rather not be privy."

Benji agreed with my assessment, so at least I wasn't coming across as paranoid as I felt.

When I called Mr. Garrett and asked him if he'd enjoy an evening stroll, he sounded delighted. He must have known there was another motive behind the invitation, but he didn't let on.

Fifteen minutes later we were walking past the outdoor movie. It was just beginning, and a few guests were starting to trickle in.

"So, what is the real reason for this walk?" Mr. Garrett asked after we were out of earshot from anyone. The path that wound its way through the golf course was lined with small solar lanterns, and they cast unnerving shadows around us.

"We need to know more about Mark's brother, Robert," I said.

Mr. Garrett nodded, like he'd been expecting this question to come up eventually.

"He's a likable fellow. Has a way of getting you to agree to do things before you realize what you're getting yourself into, and then uses his expertise as a lawyer to make sure you can't back out of it."

I thought back to how Robert had gotten me to agree to investigate Mark's murder. He hadn't threatened me, though, and had been nothing but pleasant. And why would he ask me to investigate if he was the one who had done it?

"So, he's terrifying, then?" Benji asked.

"Very," Mr. Garrett agreed. "And I know what you're thinking—that Robert is the murderer. I had the same thought, considering how contentious Robert and Mark's relationship was. But Robert has an airtight alibi. And he has no real motive. Brothers fight. It's not that unusual."

"Depends on what they were fighting about," I said.

Mr. Garrett paused on the path and looked out toward White Sands. The moon wasn't quite high enough to reflect off the sand yet, and from the sounds of tuning instruments, the concert hadn't started yet either.

"Robert's involvement with the company."

Although Robert had claimed there was no involvement on his end—that that was Mark's thing.

"We're hearing contradicting statements about his involvement with the firm you and Mr. Peters work at," I said. "Robert said he wasn't involved at all, but I'm hearing from others that he was."

"He *wanted* to be," Mr. Garrett said, pointing a finger at me to emphasize his statement. "For the past year, he's done some contract work for the firm here and there. More recently, Robert has been having trouble finding a job, and there was an opening for a permanent position. But the powers-that-be felt it wouldn't be wise. If Robert was given full access, some felt it could be an ethical dilemma if anything were to arise that involved either his father or brother. And Mark made it clear that he thought it was the correct choice. That made Robert furious. And then Nick and I decided to leave the company, and Robert saw his chance. Asked his dad for a job at the new firm."

"Let me guess," I said. "Mr. Peters said no."

Mr. Garrett tapped his nose, indicating that I'd guessed correctly. "And Robert hasn't spoken to his father or Mark since. He was under the impression that Nick and Mark were forming some sort of alliance. Was even coming up with conspiracy theories that Mark was trying to get Robert cut out of their father's will. Nick wasn't even sure that Robert would show up to the wedding." He released a long breath. "I'll admit that Mark had always had a better relationship with his father than Robert had, but I wouldn't say it was good. I mean, Nick was trying to hide the fact that Mark wouldn't be coming to the new firm until the very last second. He knew everything was going to blow up when that came out."

Okay, the whole family had issues. Got it.

"You say that Robert had an airtight alibi?" Because the more I heard about the elder brother, the more I was convinced that he had to have done this. Yes, others had motive. But Robert had the temperament for it.

"Robert was at the wedding with the rest of the guests. Only left for a couple of minutes to take a phone call, but he couldn't have gone far. Certainly not all the way up to the fifth floor, and definitely not out to White Sands."

I assumed that had already been verified with security footage. I'd have to look at the videos Flash had sent me. Again.

Mr. Garrett glanced at his watch. "Sorry to cut this short, but my wife will be wondering what's taking so long. She advised me not to put myself in the middle of things and doesn't know I am meeting with you. Don't let that stop you from letting me know if you need anything else, though."

Benji and I said goodbye and watched as Mr. Garrett hurried down the path, past a long row of parked golf carts, and around the corner of the resort.

"So, what do you think?" Benji asked.

Without hesitation, I said, "I don't know how, but Robert killed his brother."

"How are you going to prove that?"

I looked up at Benji. "No clue."

20

I paced across the grass, needing the cool air to keep me alert and focused.

Robert had been at the wedding. He couldn't have gone upstairs to kill Mark, then sneaked the body out to White Sands. He had then asked if I would find Mark's killer, as if he was concerned about his younger brother. I saw now that it had all been an act, meant to keep himself out of my crosshairs. Once he'd heard of my reputation, he'd realized he needed to keep me close. I couldn't believe I'd been so gullible.

But how had he managed it? How had he killed Mark?

"It wasn't possible," I said. If only I could believe that Amanda had done it. Life would be so much easier.

Benji was sitting on a bench on the edge of the path. "Did Amanda or Bree rent a golf cart?" he asked.

I'd been so focused on Robert, I hadn't even thought to

check for anyone else that he could have been working with. Another oversight on my part. I was losing my touch. At least maybe now people would stop asking me to investigate murders, and I'd stop feeling an obligation to.

"What time does the golf shop close?" I asked, glancing at my phone.

Benji stood and turned toward the hotel. He glanced back and motioned for me to join him. "Only one way to find out."

The shop was just closing as we arrived, and as the lights turned off, I gave a quick knock on the door.

An employee appeared from around the counter and pointed to the CLOSED sign. Thankfully it was a different person than I'd pestered earlier, or we might not get very far.

"Please, we just need to ask you a question," I said loudly, unsure if she could hear me.

She hesitated but then unlocked the door and opened it a crack. "I'm sorry, but I can't sell you anything past closing hours. We will open back up at seven tomorrow morning."

"That's all right, I don't need to purchase anything," I said quickly, hoping to get my explanation out before the employee shut the door again. "I just need to know if one of my friends rented a golf cart yesterday."

"Or a sled," Benji added.

A sled would provide an easier way to transport the body. Though I had to admit, it would be a bit obvious.

The employee looked annoyed, like we were equivalent to a party of ten who showed up at a restaurant five minutes before closing. But she quickly covered it, because this was a high-end resort and they were expected to treat the guests well. Far better than we'd been treated at the motel we'd stayed at for the hot air balloon festival, anyway.

"I'm sorry, but we really are closed," she said. "You could always ask your friends."

She started to close the door, and I had to think quickly, because the woman had a point. That would have been the sensible thing to do if my intentions had been as pure as I was trying to make them out to be.

"The thing is," I looked at her name tag, "Connie, my friends went sledding yesterday, and I haven't been able to get ahold of them all day. I'm worried they are still out there. I just need to see if they returned their golf cart and sled."

Connie paused, and I wondered if she'd notice that I'd changed my story and was no longer interested if they had rented the items but if they had returned them.

But maybe because a dead body had been discovered at White Sands the day before, the resort's employees were now paranoid. Because rather than look skeptical about my story, Connie looked worried.

"We would have noticed if someone had kept their rentals overnight, but I'd be happy to check for you," she said, opening the door wider and gesturing for us to enter.

"Guests aren't supposed to take the golf carts off the resort's property, but people do it all the time. It's too tempting not too, considering how big White Sands is."

Connie walked behind the counter and pulled out a binder, then looked at me expectantly, like she was waiting for something. Oh, right. My friends' names.

"Can you try Amanda? This would have been yesterday afternoon."

"What is her last name?" Connie asked, flipping a few pages in the binder.

That was a very good question. And one that I didn't know the answer to.

"Um…just Amanda."

Connie raised an eyebrow.

"She's a friend of a friend," Benji added.

After studying us for another moment, Connie turned her attention back to her binder. "Okay. Just Amanda." She ran her finger along the sheet of paper. Then another. Then one more. "I'm not seeing anyone with that name."

I hadn't expected her to.

"Bree Garrett?" I tried.

Connie turned back a few pages. "Nope. Not for her either."

Thank goodness. I could see the relief wash over Benji.

"Looks like they must have skipped out on White Sands yesterday," Connie continued. "The cell phone service out here isn't great, so I'm not surprised you haven't been able to get ahold of them. Try one of the top floors, you'll have better luck. The ninth floor works best for me."

Good thing that was where we were staying. Now we could call our fictional friends who we were so worried about. There must have been someone else who could have rented the cart. Maybe the vending machine guy. What was his name?

"They have another friend," I said, my tone bordering on desperate. "Try Kent. Or maybe an employee drove them out and dropped them off."

Yeah, that had to be it. The murderer didn't want a record of them taking out the cart, so they'd had an employee take them out.

An employee had driven Robert out with a bag big enough to hold a body?

I had officially lost my mind.

Connie closed the binder, indicating that our time together was finished. "Employees aren't allowed to take the golf carts. Maintenance has their own transportation, and no one else has need of them. Now, if you'll excuse me, my boss will freak out if he sees you guys in here."

I didn't want to leave, but Benji ushered me out while thanking Connie for her help.

"You tried. There was nothing more you could have done," Benji said, his tone soft. If anything, it only made me feel worse.

I had failed.

Amanda would go to jail, whether she had committed the murder or not.

"I don't understand," I said.

"Isn't it possible that Robert isn't the killer? That Amanda really did do it?"

Possible? Of course. But not likely.

"Why can't we find proof? It's like Robert is a ghost. He's only appeared exactly as he wanted to, playing the part of the perfect brother the entire time he's been here. He's been where he's supposed to be, appearing on all the right cameras. No one else has managed that. Everyone else has been in exactly the wrong place at the wrong time." I paused, realization setting in. "That's how I know he did it."

But it still didn't explain how.

"It's possible he didn't bother to ask to take the golf cart," Benji said. "The keys for those things aren't like car keys—one set could fit all of the carts. And then, of course, he could have just used a screwdriver to start it up. Easiest thing in the world."

I'd need to ask Benji how he knew how to steal a golf cart later.

Because right now, I felt sick.

My heart landed in my shoes as images cascaded over me, each clicking into place to form a complete picture.

I knew who had killed Mark.

21

I stood in the security office, bouncing on my toes, anxious for this to all be over.

"You're sure about this?" Benji whispered in my ear. "Because if you're wrong—"

"I'm not wrong," I said, cutting off his words. Doing this —making these accusations—it didn't make me happy. I didn't want to be here.

But I knew I was right.

The detective walked in, his lips pulled into a frown. "Ms. Swallows, if you're wrong about this—"

"I'm not wrong," I half-yelled, startling both the detective and Benji. My nerves were getting the best of me, and I forced myself to take a deep breath. "I'm not wrong," I said more quietly.

The detective gave a small nod. "I don't like that you've injected yourself into this investigation, but I can't afford to ignore you if it means an innocent woman would go to jail."

"I understand," I said. "And trust me, this was not how I envisioned this weekend playing out either."

The head of security, Carlos, stuck his head into the office. "Robert Peters is here."

Detective Holbrook turned to me and raised an eyebrow. "How does this thing play out? Do we bring them in together? Separately?"

Chances were they'd already talked to get their story straight, so separate might not produce any results. Unless we lied about what the other had told us, then got them to turn on each other.

But my inner psychologist was telling me that together was going to give us the biggest bang for our buck. And I meant that literally. Robert couldn't keep his cool persona together for much longer—not if he was as explosive as others had said he was. At this point, he must be practically bursting at the seams.

And we were going to rip that seam wide open.

"Together," I said.

Benji laid a hand on my arm. "You're sure that's wise?"

No, I wasn't sure about a thing, except that I wanted this to be over with.

"Together," I repeated.

Detective Holbrook nodded toward the doorway. "Bring them both in."

Carlos looked to me, then the detective, as if he was

unsure who was giving orders around here. "Only Robert is here. The other should be arriving any moment."

"Does Robert know that we know?" I asked.

"No," Carlos said. "He thinks it's more routine questioning. Can't say he's happy about it either."

"Keep it that way, and show him in, please," I said.

Carlos glanced at Detective Holbrook, his eyes seemingly asking if that was okay.

The detective gave a little nod, and Carlos disappeared.

"I hope you know what you're doing," the detective muttered.

So did I, considering that I didn't know what Robert was capable of when he got angry. Or desperate. Other than murder, of course. And I was afraid we were about to find out.

"Carlos is a big guy. He can handle Robert," I said.

Detective Holbrook smirked. "We'll see."

And then Robert appeared in the doorway, and I knew the moment he'd spotted me.

Gone was the easy smile he'd always had for me. The cool confidence. His eyes flashed in anger.

And just as quickly, his smile was firmly back in place as he walked into the room. It was so fast that I doubted anyone else had noticed. But his gaze was more guarded now as he took in the detective, with Benji and me at his sides.

"We having a town hall meeting?" Robert joked.

Detective Holbrook humored him with a small smile. "Something like that."

"All right." Robert sat down in the chair across from the detective and settled in. His smile had grown wider—too wide to be natural. As if he was overcompensating for something. "What's on the agenda today?"

"Your brother's murder," Detective Holbrook said. "As usual."

Robert seemed to stiffen, and with it, he sat up a little straighter. "You finally got that woman to confess?"

Detective Holbrook was quiet for longer than necessary as he studied Robert. I had to admit, I was impressed with his skills. Robert was shifting uncomfortably under his gaze, as if he'd rather be anywhere else.

"No, Amanda did not confess," the detective finally said. "And frankly, I'm beginning to have my doubts she had anything to do with it at all." He paused. "We need a new angle on this thing."

Robert's calm composure faltered. "You can't let her go," he said, struggling to keep his voice even. "Not unless you have someone else in handcuffs. My brother's death cannot go unpunished."

"We completely agree."

Robert glanced at Benji and me. "Since when does your investigation include these two? If it's all the same, I'd rather if you stuck with professional law enforcement. You know, people who know what they're doing."

My pulse quickened and my face felt hot with anger,

considering that just that morning Robert had been begging me to help solve his brother's death.

Benji touched my hand lightly, and I interpreted it as him asking me to be patient. To not lose my cool.

Thankfully, I was saved from having to use self-restraint, because our second guest finally arrived.

And rather than giving Robert the satisfaction of seeing me lose my temper, I smiled.

But it was forced.

Because I hated what we were about to do.

The detective turned to where my gaze had landed. "Hello, Elijah. I'm unsure if we've met. I'm Detective Holbrook." He gestured to the empty seat next to Robert. Please, come in."

A lot happened at once in those next few seconds.

Elijah had frozen in the doorway, his gaze jumping to each of us in the room. He looked like he wanted to turn around and run, but Carlos was standing directly behind him.

Robert had also frozen, as if he couldn't believe we might have been smart enough to figure things out. His expression was panicked, and then it morphed into anger, then back to panic, like he was trying to figure out how to play this. It finally settled on cool indif-ference.

"I'm sorry, I really don't have time for this," Elijah said, his voice squeaking out. He cleared his throat and tried again. "We have a lot of guests just arriving, and I'm needed to help with their luggage. The resort has a reputation to uphold, you know."

"This will only take a few minutes," Detective Holbrook said. "Please, sit."

Elijah didn't move.

Robert grunted. "Oh, let the boy go do his job. Surely you can call him in later."

Detective Holbrook glanced at me, his eyes asking what I'd like to do.

"Elijah, you need us," I said, my voice soft. "Robert will do to you what he had you do to his brother. We can protect you. And your mother."

That struck a nerve.

Elijah's eyes widened. Maybe he hadn't thought that his involvement with this might put his mother in danger. His motivation had likely been the opposite. He gave a quick nod and scurried in, but he didn't sit next to Robert as he threw frightened glances his way. He instead chose to stand against the back wall, stiff, with his hands clasped nervously in front of him.

A tense silence settled over the room, and I wondered what the detective's next move would be.

It ended up being Robert who spoke first. "I don't have time for this." He moved to stand.

"Then make the time," Carlos barked from the doorway. "Because you ain't leaving this room until the detective says you can, and even then, it's going to be in handcuffs."

This time Robert didn't bother to mask his fury. "How dare you accuse me of murdering my brother. I loved Mark, and I did not kill him. You have no proof otherwise."

The man thought he was untouchable, that he'd thought of every little detail. And he had. The man was certainly a good lawyer, because he had made sure there hadn't been any holes in his defense.

Except for one small problem.

"But we do have evidence of you paying Elijah to do it for you," I said. "And he admitted to it all, so you might as well make things easier for yourself."

Evidence was a bit of an exaggeration. I had a strong hunch that had led to some firm beliefs. And an assumption that Elijah would go along with my story, because he was a good kid who had been caught at a bad time by a terrible person.

"Why would you do that?" Robert roared, turning on Elijah. "You think you can help your mother if you're in prison? Did you think about that?"

Elijah's decision to not sit next to Robert had been wise. He couldn't retreat any further, so he pressed himself into the wall, as if that would help put more distance between them.

"I didn't say anything," he whimpered.

Okay, my assumption that Elijah would go along with my plan had been off. But I knew I was on the right track, so I kept pushing.

"That's a heartless thing to do," I said to Robert.

"Taking advantage of a desperate young man whose only fault is loving his mother so much that he would kill for her." It didn't sound all that great when I said it out loud.

Detective Holbrook held up a hand. "Whoa, whoa, whoa. I thought you were bringing in Elijah as a witness. You're saying that he is the one who killed Mark?" His expression was as baffled as I'd felt when the thought had first come to me. "To what end?"

I looked at Elijah and was heartbroken by his moist eyes and the fear etched in his features. "Would you like to tell the detective, or would you rather I do it?" I asked him gently.

Elijah sniffled and scooted along the wall so there was more space between him and Robert. "You can do it."

"Correct me if I get anything wrong, though, okay?"

Elijah nodded.

I turned back to the detective. "Robert was convinced that his brother had turned their parents against him. Thought he was being left out of the company, the will... everything. He hadn't seen them for ages, and attending the wedding might have been his only chance to rectify things."

The detective still looked confused. "Okay, I understand what Robert could gain from his brother being dead. But I don't see what Elijah has to do with anything."

I stole another glance at Elijah. His head was bowed, tears now making tracks down his cheeks. "Elijah is a talker. He enjoys connecting with guests—it's the reason he's so good at his job. But he tried connecting with the wrong man. Must have mentioned that he was working extra shifts to pay for his mother's surgery that she was in desperate need of. But even working extra shifts at a luxury resort, it was going to take years for Elijah to make the money he needed, and I'm guessing his mother doesn't have that kind of time."

When I looked at Elijah, he nodded in affirmation.

"So, Robert offered to pay Elijah to do a job for him. That way, he could keep his hands clean," Detective Holbrook guessed.

"This is preposterous," Robert growled, and angrily pushed back his chair. "The young man obviously has some mental issues and is now trying to pin the blame on me. Well, I'm not going to sit around and listen to it for another minute longer." But when Robert tried leaving, Carlos blocked his way.

"You can sit down and listen, or you can do it in hand-cuffs," he said, his features twisted in disgust. "Elijah is a good kid. Better than you'll ever be. Heck, better than *I'll* ever be. And it isn't right, the position you put him in."

Robert lifted his hands in a defensive gesture and took a step back. "Look, I never forced him to do anything."

"No," I said. "You only gave him the choice between his mother's life or Mark's. And I already know Elijah's feelings about Mark. He was not a man that would be missed by Elijah, or anyone else, for that matter. And Elijah would do anything to save his mother."

"Even kill?" the detective asked, his voice soft.

We all looked to Elijah. He didn't return our gazes but he gave another little nod.

Detective Holbrook looked astounded by the admission, and he turned to me. "How did you know? Because even with this new information, the logistics still don't make any sense to me. The wedding was postponed last minute, which he wouldn't have known."

"Yes, the last-minute change of plans did throw a kink in things, didn't it?" I asked Robert. He merely glared, but I hadn't actually expected an answer. "Robert had chosen Elijah because of his desperate family situation, but also because Elijah could go anywhere in the resort and no one would bat an eye. He'd been working, not just luggage, but also housekeeping, and anything else the resort was in need of. They were desperate for any help they could get. Which meant that it wouldn't be difficult for Elijah to sneak into the groom's room next to the venue and kill Mark there. Hence, the cake knife."

"But Mark wasn't there," the detective guessed.

"Nope. If you check Robert's phone records, I'll bet anything that the phone call he took just before the wedding was from Elijah, telling him about the problem."

The detective was slowly catching on. "So, when an anonymous caller told us that someone had been murdered..."

"It was Robert. If the hotel's employees have to check every room for signs of trouble, it would take all hands on deck. Including Elijah. Amanda told me that the bellhop had quickly checked in on her but that he was next door for several minutes before he left. Elijah had nothing good to say about Mark, and now the guy was drunk, depressed, and angry. Why would Elijah spend any more time there than necessary?"

"We had noticed on the cameras that it was a man checking the rooms on that floor," Detective Holbrook said slowly, like he was finally starting to believe me. "Didn't think anything of it because we could tell he was an employee and he was pushing around that big laundry basket."

Benji hadn't said anything up until this point, his gaze firmly fixed on his feet. When I had shared my realizations with him before visiting the hotel security office, he hadn't wanted to believe it. I hadn't either.

"Tell them about the laundry basket," Benji said, his voice quiet.

I gave a little nod and hoped I could do it without having to bring up how I just so happened to know what had been on the security cameras, when I obviously shouldn't.

"Like you had noticed, when Elijah went up to check on everyone, he was pushing one of those large rolling laundry baskets they use for dirty linens."

Detective Holbrook shrugged. "Sure. Figured it was to make it look as if he was just passing through on his way to clean a room."

"Did you also notice it looking fuller, and heavier, after visiting Mark's room?"

By posing it as a question, the detective thought I was simply inquiring rather than making a statement. Which was good because this was something I certainly shouldn't know.

And I doubted he'd believe me if I told him I hadn't asked for those security videos to be sent to me. They had been forced on me. Honest.

"That...is something I'll double-check," he said, his words slow, like he was annoyed with himself for not noticing it earlier.

Benji glanced over, nodding, urging me to continue.

Gladly, anything to get this over with. Not just because it was a lot of information, but also because the longer we talked, the worse Elijah seemed to be doing. He'd gone from leaning against the back wall to sliding down it and sitting on the floor, his knees pulled into his chest, much like a little boy who'd been asked to sit in the corner.

I too felt like I needed to sit down, but instead I straightened, because I needed to finish what I'd started, no matter how unpleasant it was.

"Elijah finished with the other rooms on the floor, then took the laundry basket downstairs, where he loaded Mark into a golf cart that he wasn't supposed to take."

Elijah popped his head up from where he had rested it on his knees, looking surprised. "How did you know about that? I didn't check it out or anything."

I gave Elijah a sad smile and kept my voice gentle. "Only maintenance workers are allowed their own transportation, and theirs don't look the same as the guest carts. I was told that employees aren't allowed to use them, and I know you're a stickler for rules. Wouldn't even come inside my hotel room to give me a blanket." I paused, a realization settling over me. I couldn't believe I hadn't thought of it sooner. "When we were on the fifth floor, you were just coming out of Robert's room. Something you refused to do with Benji and me." The image of Elijah patting down his pockets and smoothing his uniform came to mind. "That was when Robert paid you."

Elijah looked both frightened and impressed. "Yes, ma'am. Everything I needed for my mother's surgery."

Robert spun toward the bellhop, and Carlos hurried forward, ready to restrain the man if he needed to. "And now, because you don't have a backbone, it was all for nothing. Didn't I warn you?"

Elijah burst into sobs, and I had to fight the urge to rush over and place my arm around his shoulders.

"Get him out of here," Detective Holbrook growled, an angry gaze fixed on Robert. "My men are waiting outside."

His gaze turned softer when it settled on Elijah. "I'm sorry to say that I'll need to take you in too."

"It's okay," Elijah said, struggling to his feet. "I deserve it. Even if my mother is worth ten of that Mark guy."

"Did Robert coerce you at all? Threaten you?" the detective asked. "Did you do it under duress?"

Elijah hesitated. "No, just desperation."

And then Elijah was escorted out.

"I feel for the kid, I really do," the detective said. "He's not a killer."

I was tempted to say the same. But it wasn't true. Elijah was a good kid when he was in good circumstances. But this showed that unbearable amounts of stress could make him do things he wouldn't normally.

And life was full of large amounts of stress.

As much as I hated to admit it, Elijah was dangerous. As was Robert.

And we'd done a good thing today.

22

Benji and I exited the hotel and stepped into the night air. After leaving the security office, I couldn't imagine returning to our room. The large hotel was suddenly stifling, and I needed space. A lot of it.

"Hold up there." Detective Holbrook followed us out.

I turned, holding my breath. I'd thought we were finished with all this.

"Something we can do for you?" Benji asked, his tone defensive.

The detective held up both hands. "I'm not here to arrest anyone. Just wanted to thank you. I'm not so stubborn that I don't admit when I've made a mistake."

"In all fairness," I said, "I would have come to the same conclusion you did, given the evidence."

Detective Holbrook raised an eyebrow. "And yet, you didn't."

I couldn't fight a small smile. "No, but only because luck was on my side."

"Smart *and* humble. A rare combination," he said, matching my smile. Now that he wasn't stressed out, he looked like someone Benji and I might have been friends with, under different circumstances.

"Anything else you need?" Benji interjected. He looked antsy, like he wanted nothing more than to never see Detective Holbrook again.

The detective's smile faded, and he took on an air of professionalism. "Um, yes. Of course. My officers are in the process of releasing Amanda and preparing the other two for transport in the morning. We have all their personal possessions, but there is the matter of the money that Robert paid for Mark's murder. It seems it has disappeared. Considering Elijah doesn't live at the hotel, his locker was empty, and it's not on his person, I'm going on the assumption that he must have given it to someone. A friend, perhaps."

I attempted to look perplexed, but with my acting skills, I knew it wasn't going to fool anyone. "Oh, is that right? Very strange. I wish you the best of luck with that." The envelope sat heavy in my jacket pocket, and I forced myself to not look down. Elijah must have a side gig as a magician because I'd had no idea it was even there until we'd already left the office. It had come with a name and an address scribbled on the outside.

The detective hesitated. "In your professional opinion,

is it a safe assumption that the money will somehow make its way into the hands of Elijah's mother?"

I pretended to think about the question before answering. "Yes, I think it is."

"Good," Detective Holbrook said. "The poor woman is going to suffer enough with her son in prison. I'd hate to think we'd taken away this too." And then he disappeared back through the doors, leaving Benji and me alone once more.

We stared after him long after he was gone, not speaking. But what was there to say? As for me, I was grateful there were still decent people in the world.

Benji turned back toward the path that would lead us through the golf course, and I followed.

We walked in comfortable silence until we reached the fence that separated the resort from White Sands National Park. I stopped, sucked in a long breath, and tilted my face up to the sky.

The investigation was finally over.

I didn't love the outcome. I worried for Elijah.

But the fear was gone. The dread. The anxiety of the unknown.

"You doing okay?" Benji asked, breaking the quiet.

When my gaze lowered, it was just him, the starry sky, and nothing else.

My heart quickened, and I finally understood, embarrassed that it had taken me so long to figure it out.

I finally understood that nothing else mattered.

Whatever was going on in my life, Benji had always been there. And always would be. He was my best friend. Whatever baggage we both had, it was inconsequential.

And I'd much rather go through life—murder accusations included—with him than without.

I deserved a good life and a good man. My kids deserved it too.

Words eluded me, and so, I answered Benji in the only way I knew how.

I kissed him.

I could tell that I had surprised Benji, and it took him a moment to react. But then he pulled me in close, his arms wrapping around my waist. I placed my hands on the back of his neck, relishing every touch and every shuddered sigh.

Because it had been a long time coming.

I didn't want to pull away—didn't want it to end. But end it did.

When we finally separated, our breaths were quick. And the realization of what we'd just done crashed over me.

I had kissed Benji. My best friend.

I was grateful for the dark because I could feel heat rushing into my cheeks. I couldn't even look Benji in the eyes.

What if he regretted it? Would this make things weird between us? We had a whole night ahead of us still. Maybe

I shouldn't have kissed him. Or should have at least waited until I could make a quick getaway. Just in case things went south.

But then Benji placed a finger under my chin and lifted it so that my gaze met his.

He was smiling, so that was a good sign.

My heart pounded so fast, it felt like it would burst from my chest.

"I've been waiting a long time for that kiss," he said, his lips quirked up into a teasing smile. "Over thirty years."

Confusion settled over me. "But you dated all those girls in high school, and then there was—"

Benji stopped my words with another kiss.

I let him stop them for another few minutes before pulling away and wondering why I'd waited so long for this moment.

And then I remembered. "You know, it wasn't just me that was keeping us from that kiss. This past year, anytime I got too close, you pulled away."

Benji's smile dipped, and I wondered if kissing him again would bring it back. "I know I've been conflicted, and that hasn't been fair to you. One minute I'm telling you that I want to take things further, and then the next moment I'm...not." He blew out a hard breath. "There's been a lot of guilt."

"Because of Candace?" I guessed.

He gave a slight nod. "Partially. But mostly because I'm

moving on to the one person I've always loved. Even when I was dating Candace, I knew that if you walked into town, I'd drop everything to be with you. This weekend, after watching the way Mark and his family had torn themselves apart and how awful Bree and Mark's relationship had been—I don't have time for guilt. Especially guilt for things I cannot change."

Benji took my hands in his, and my breath hitched. "I love you, Maddie. This weekend...I had high hopes. And then everything came crashing down around us, and I worried that that was what our relationship was destined to be. One disaster after another, and us just trying to get to the other side of it."

A grin erupted across my forty-two-year-old face, and I felt like I was fourteen again. Benji loved me.

"I know things have been crazy since I returned to Amor. But there's no one else in the world I'd rather traverse life's disasters with. Because I love you too, Benji." At my confession, a sense of euphoria crashed over me, threatening to drown me. I'd always loved Benji. But I was finally admitting that I was *in love* with Benji. I quickly added, "And I promise, I'll try to keep the murder investigations down to a minimum. I can't guarantee anything, but I'll try."

"And that's all a guy can ask for," he said, returning my smile.

A weight lifted off me, and I felt more at peace with life than I had in a very long time.

"I think the concert's still going," I said, tilting my head and catching a few stray notes floating on the breeze. I slipped my hand into Benji's. "Care to join me?"

He squeezed my hand. "I'd like nothing more."

EPILOGUE

Benji held out a spoonful of spaghetti sauce toward me. "Did I get the spices right?"

I'd been breaking noodles into a large pot of water and stepped to the side, just out of his reach. "You know I can't eat sauce on its own. Not until everything is all together. Trish will try it, though."

Ava, our cat, had somehow ended up nestled between Benji's feet, and he had to avoid stepping on her as he turned toward where my roommate was setting the salad on the table. From the day that Ava and I had met, she had taken it upon herself to whack me any chance she got, but for Benji, she was all purrs.

Until now. He accidentally stepped on her tail as he shifted his feet, and she let out a scream while swiping at him with her claws. As Benji was jumping out of the way and apologizing, another screech echoed through the house. This one had come from upstairs.

Lilly.

"Mom," she shouted. Her voice had an urgency that wasn't normally there.

I rushed out of the kitchen and took the steps two at a time, with Benji and Trish close behind.

When I burst into Lilly's bedroom, she released another scream, which in turn caused me to scream.

"What's wrong?" I asked, panicked.

Lilly was bent over, a hand to her chest. "You scaring the heck out of me, that's what's wrong. Why can't you enter my room like a normal person?"

Now that I'd had time to catch my breath and take things in, I didn't sense any danger. Nothing out of place. "Because you sounded like something was wrong. I thought you'd cut yourself or someone had broken in or—"

Lilly held up a hand and started laughing. "I'm freaking out because I submitted a photograph to a competition run by the spaceport. And I won! They want me out there when the inaugural space tourism flight lands to take pictures of the event. And if they like the photos enough, they are open to further collaboration."

And that would mean that my daughter, who I still couldn't quite think of as an adult, wouldn't be leaving me quite yet. The spaceport was close enough that it wouldn't make sense for her to move out.

I joined her for additional happy screaming.

"This is a huge opportunity," Benji said. "Who knows all the doors it could open for you." He paused, a knowing glint in his eye. "Even a documentary."

Lilly paused her excited freakout for a moment, her eyes bright. "I hadn't thought of that. I better sign up for the documentary class I've been wanting to take." And she jumped into her computer chair, pulling up the website for an online film school that she'd been eyeing for several months.

She glanced back at me. "Oh, and Mom, they said that they'd appreciate it if you and Trish would respond to the emails they've been sending you. And they asked for your phone numbers. Apparently, the spaceport has been trying to contact you for a few weeks now. When they made the connection that I was your daughter, they asked that I pass on the message."

Emails?

Realization settled in. Oh. *Those* emails.

The ones that Trish and I had deleted, assuming we'd landed on someone's scam list. The ones saying they were from Galactic Enterprises' Space Tourism Experience. We'd joked that the *Star Trek* convention was trying to recruit us.

Trish and I shared guilty looks.

"What is it exactly that they want?" Trish asked.

"Something about doing contract work with you whenever they have a flight," Lilly said. "Sounds like the tourists are here for a few days of training before going up into space, and they would like a psychologist to be on hand to help them through the experience. All you really need to know to make your decision is that you're going to meet tons of celebrities." She released a sigh. "You're so lucky."

Trish and I were already so busy between our regular patients and visiting the homeless community. But the spaceport...that was an opportunity I wasn't sure I could give up.

"What do you think?" I asked Trish.

She hesitated, but from the excited gleam in her eyes, I could tell she really wanted to do it. "It would probably only be once every few months. We could take turns going out there so that we'd always have someone here holding down the fort. First flight probably isn't for a while anyway."

Lilly held up a hand, like she was in class.

"Yes, Lilly?" I said with an amused smile.

"It's in three weeks."

Oh. That was soon.

I felt something soft rub against my legs and looked down to see Ava rubbing against me, a soft purr accompanying it.

My gaze snapped up to Benji, my eyes wide. Ava never showed me any affection.

"Looks like she's giving her opinion," he said.

When I'd decided to move my family down to Amor, I'd never imagined it working out like this.

But here I was with a successful business that I ran with my best friend, two amazing kids, and a boyfriend I couldn't love more.

And now I'd been asked to help celebrities prepare themselves mentally to go into space.

I knew that I could handle the job, and I couldn't wait to get started.

Assuming no dead bodies showed up.

The End

ALSO BY KAT BELLEMORE

MADDIE SWALLOWS MYSTERY SERIES

Dead Before Dinner

Dead Upon Arrival

Dead Before I Do

Dead Upon Arrival

BORROWING AMOR

Borrowing Amor

Borrowing Love

Borrowing a Fiancé

Borrowing a Billionaire

Borrowing Kisses

Borrowing Second Chances

STARLIGHT RIDGE

Diving into Love

Resisting Love

Starlight Love

Building on Love

Winning his Love

Returning to Love

ABOUT THE AUTHOR

Kat Bellemore is the author of both the Borrowing Amor small town romance series and the Maddie Swallows cozy mystery series. Deciding to have New Mexico as the setting for these series was an easy choice, considering its amazing sunsets, blue skies and tasty green chile. That, and she currently lives there with her husband and two cute kids. They hope to one day add a dog to the family, but for now, the native animals of the desert will have to do. Though, Kat wouldn't mind ridding the world of scorpions and centipedes. They're just mean.

You can visit Kat at www.kat-bellemore.com.